Cooper: Cl

M000306718

Romance, cowboys, rodeo, ranching and wild mustangs...the Presley men, aka the cowboys of Ransom Creek, will win your heart and have you longing for Texas.

After making a major dating mistake, Cooper Presley has sworn off women. But then he meets his new neighbor and she's making his new "no dating policy" hard to abide by. She's special and he knows it, but what's he going to do about it?

Beth Lee is happy to settle into her new property with her baby goats and her dreams of a small productive farm. Forced to hide from her ex-boyfriend, she isn't looking for romance of any kind. Especially with a cowboy with a jealous ex of his own. But after Cooper rescues her baby goats she can't get the handsome cowboy off her mind.

When her past catches up to her, Cooper Presley

comes to her rescue. Now, despite all the rumors and the jealous ex's, Beth is at risk of falling in love with the sexy cowboy.

The small town of Ransom Creek is buzzing with rumors, a little suspense…and a lot of speculation that Cooper Presley might be the first of those handsome Presley men to fall in love.

COOPER:
CHARMED BY THE COWBOY

Cowboys of Ransom Creek, Book Three

DEBRA
CLOPTON

Cooper: Charmed by the Cowboy

Copyright © 2018 Debra Clopton Parks

CHAPTER ONE

Moving cautiously down the ravine, Beth Lee stumbled over a tree root and would have careened down the steep incline if she hadn't grabbed the branch of a yaupon bush just in time. Breathing hard, she clung to her flimsy lifeline as her boots fought for traction on the soft dirt. The steep ravine looming before her, she could feel the ground giving way beneath her. She grabbed for more hand holds-this was not going to be good if she took this fall. Desperation seized her and she tightened her grip on the branches as she finally caught her balance on semisolid ground.

She breathed a sigh of relief and remained completely still, testing her precarious position before taking the next step down the ravine.

She'd been traipsing around in this pasture—*pastures*, she corrected herself because she'd walked for over two hours and had crawled through a couple of barbed wire fences in the process. She'd finally come upon this woodsy, steep ravine cutting through her neighbor's huge ranch. She'd walked along this one side, calling Tilly's name, and now she was attempting to cross to the other side. In hopes that maybe little Tilly was hiding under a bush or, if she'd traveled this far, maybe she was under a bush sleeping or…Beth didn't want to think about her being out here hurt.

Panic clutched at her as she pushed forward. So far, all she'd found was buzzing insects, creepy rustling in the underbrush, that had her very thankful she was wearing her boots—and had her jeans tucked into them. The last thing she wanted was a snake racing up her pants legs. The thought sent a shiver up her spine.

Enough.

"Tilly," she called again, her throat scratchy from all the yelling she'd done.

Poor Tilly. She was probably scared, but hopefully okay. Goats were surefooted—even baby goats like Tilly.

Which was more than she could say for herself. Taking a cautious step, she moved to walk parallel to the drop-off. She needed to find a good place to climb down and then across so that she could go to the other side. The only problem was, if Tilly hadn't gone across but instead had followed the small stream at the bottom of the ravine, who knew where she was. She might never find the baby goat. This was the Presley Ranch. It was huge, at least by her standards. She thought her uncle Howard had said it was about eight thousand acres. His place, hers for now, was a mere forty acres surrounded on all sides by this ranch, so the difference was significant.

"Tilly," she called, as she'd been doing off and on since the goat had disappeared and she'd followed tiny hoof marks this way as far as they'd been visible. "*Tilly*," she called, again. Her heart thundered as she heard the unmistakable howl of a coyote sounding behind her. Close behind her.

Beth swung around—immediately she lost her balance and plunged down the very steep, rough embankment.

She might have screamed, might have groaned and gasped. She wasn't really sure as she finally landed with a thud, bounced then rolled and landed on her butt, sitting up in the mud beside the trickling brook that cut through the bottom of the ravine.

"Great," she groaned, looking upward through the tall canopy of trees. She had rolled through a mass of underbrush to get to this muddy spot. But, looking on the bright side, the mud had broken her fall.

She carefully shifted to her knees.

Her ankle ached but considering the path she'd just blazed down like a wrecking ball, it was a miracle she hadn't broken something—*like her neck*. She'd been lucky and seemed okay.

Other than the fact that she was alone out here at

the bottom of this ravine and no one knew it, this could have been bad. Very bad, when she reached in her pocket for her phone only to realize that in her haste to find Tilly she'd left her phone sitting on the workbench in the barn. If she'd been hurt badly she would have had no way to get help.

Feeling very isolated, she was pushing to her feet when the coyote howled somewhere above her. And then another one howled, sending a shiver racing through her—they sounded close.

Cooper Presley was not in the mood for trouble but the steer didn't care what kind of mood he was in as it cut from the herd and made a break for the trees. He nudged his horse to action and instantly had his rope whirling overhead. Keeping his eyes pinned on the steer, he rose slightly in the saddle and sent the loop sailing through the air...it was then that he saw the flash of red.

It bounced from the stand of yaupon bushes and into the path of the stampeding thousand pounds of rawhide and certain calamity.

What the dickens.

His stomach lurched as he thought for a second it was a toddler bouncing from the protection of the bushes into the path of the raging steer. Startled, the young steer bolted away from the red-clad form and managed to avoid wiping it out.

Cooper's mouth fell open as his forgotten rope missed its mark and fell to the ground. Relief coursed through him as he jerked his horse to a halt and gaped. Nope, if he hadn't seen it with his own eyes, he would not have believed it.

But there it stood: a tiny, white goat—*dressed in a frilly red dress.*

It pranced around and as if nothing about its appearance was odd, it blinked at him. "Baaaa," it bleated. "Baaaa."

Cooper laughed. "This is ridiculous." He scanned the area, expecting one of his four brothers—or all of them—to be hiding in the bushes, playing a practical joke on him. Probably videoing it for some strange reason. He scowled and narrowed his eyes as he sought the shadows of the woods. He saw no one.

"Baaaa," the tiny goat cried again.

Cooper stared at it. *Who in the world would do that to a goat?*

It was a small goat, but not acting like a newborn. Probably a baby dwarf goat. Those were far littler than regular-sized goats—not that he was an expert on goats; he was a cowboy, a cattleman through and through, and that did not include goat or sheep herding.

Especially if it wore a dress.

How had the young goat gotten way out here in the middle of nowhere? *Especially wearing that red dress with sparkly do-dads hanging off of it.*

Strangest thing he'd seen in a while. Maybe ever.

He squinted toward the trees, still expecting his brothers to ride out of the trees any moment. But no, not so far.

"Where did you come from?" he asked, dismounting slowly so not to send the tiny goat running again.

If his brothers were videoing this, he was going to hurt them. He bent forward and held out his hand to the animal. It leaned its small, bony face to the left and stared at him. Then it slowly leaned it to the right, keeping its eyes on him.

"You can trust me. Where did you come from, little lady? What are you doing here?" he crooned as he wiggled his fingers. To his surprise, the goat suddenly decided he was to be trusted and sprang at him, little red dress and all. He caught it against his chest and instantly had a cold nose nuzzling the crook of his neck. And then it head butted him in the chin.

"Ow." Cooper chuckled. He was used to dodging newborn calf noses and head butts and the tiny goat was more than half the size of a calf.

The dress crumpled in puffy folds around the goat's waist as he set the animal into the crook of his arm. "Where's Bo Peep?" he asked tucking the folds of the dress down.

Bo Peep—did he have that right? He thought of his mother, remembering when he was a boy, before she died. She would tell him and his brothers nursery rhymes. But he was just a boy and hadn't thought of them since he was nestled up in her arms as she read.

He hadn't thought of that memory in a long time. He'd been four when his mother died giving birth to his baby sister. He had been barely old enough to retain memories of her, much less facts from stories she read to him and his siblings. But that was more than Shane and Vance had. They'd been too young to remember practically anything and, of course, Lana had never known her. He yanked his thoughts from a past that couldn't be changed and focused on the bleating, wriggling ball of red in his arms. He stared down at the goat.

His brow dipped. *Sheep.* It had been a sheep that Bo Peep had lost. He smiled as the memory of his mother reciting the rhyme became clear in his mind.

"Well, little missy," he drawled in his best John Wayne impersonation. "I guess you're riding with me." He kept a firm grip on his new friend, stuck his boot into the stirrup and climbed back into the saddle.

"Baaa," the goat cried as Cooper took the reins. "Let's go find out who put you in this awful dress."

He decided the first place to look would be the small farm that cut into the Presley Ranch on the north side. A good ride from here but the best option. He headed that way. The owner had moved over a month ago but he'd heard that his niece was supposed to be moving in some time soon. A city girl—maybe she was responsible for doing this to this poor creature.

City folks had some really odd ideas sometimes. He looked down at the dress-wearing goat and laughed. It was odd all right.

If any of his brothers or ranch hands saw him, he knew he wouldn't hear the end of the teasing for a very long time.

As he rode over the hill, he spotted his older brother Drake ramrodding the separating of the steers. No way to get around it, he loped his horse toward Drake.

Even at a distance, he saw the instant Drake noticed he had something in his arms. He brought his horse to a halt and nudged his hat brim up with a knuckle and stared at him.

"What is *that*?" Drake eyed the animal as though it were a rattlesnake about to bite.

Cooper reined in his horse and hitched a brow.

"Haven't you ever seen a goat dressed up like it's going to Sunday school?"

"No, and never wanted to. *Who* in the world would do that to a goat?"

"Beats me." Cooper scowled. "And why would it be way out here dressed up like that is my other question."

"It's a wonder it hasn't been eaten by a coyote."

"That's what I was thinking." Cooper lifted it from the crook of his arm and held it up so Drake could get a good gander at the whole outfit. Knobby-kneed, white-haired legs dangled from beneath the red skirt of the dress and protruded from the short sleeves of the top. "It's not much more than a baby."

"Baaa," the goat cried, kicking its skinny legs.

Drake grimaced. "Goats have about the most irritating voice there is, even that size."

"Tell me about it."

"Hey, maybe this is another ploy to win your heart by sendin—"

"Don't even go there," Cooper warned.

"I'm just sayin', women and men both have used

11

dogs and babies to help get dates before. Maybe Nicole is getting creative."

"Why'd you have to go and bring her into this?"

His brother grinned, telling Cooper he was enjoying needling him. Cooper had recently sworn off dating for the foreseeable future after the fiasco he'd just been through. His brothers hadn't believed him and were enjoying teasing him.

"Couldn't help myself." Drake's eyes twinkled.

"For your information, I haven't changed my mind. I've got my blinders on where women are concerned these days. And I know you and the other *brothers* have a bet pool going."

"We don—" Drake snapped, then stopped. He wasn't one to lie and Cooper knew it. "All right, so what if we do. Brothers have to have fun and you know if one of us had said something that outrageous, you'd be in on the action too."

"Maybe so, but I'm just warning you not to bet more than you can afford to lose because I'm done. I've learned my lesson."

He knew their bets were capped at ten dollars, so

he figured every one of his five brothers were sitting at the limit on their bets. At Drake's *I'll-believe-that-when-pigs-fly* expression, Cooper frowned. "Fine. Do what you want, think what you want. I'm heading over to the Lee farm. Maybe Howard's niece moved in."

"See? Already going to see a woman." Drake looked satisfied that he'd rested his case.

Cooper didn't take the bait. "That's the closest place I can think of to this area where the goat could have come from. I'll let you know after I get there. Oh, by the way, that steer I was chasing headed down into the ravine. Good luck getting him out of that underbrush."

"Great," Drake groaned. "I'll take care of it. Good luck." He grinned. "You want me to take a picture of you with your new little friend so you can put it on social media?"

He shot daggers at his eldest brother. "You can forget you saw me."

Drake laughed as Cooper rode off. "I don't think you and your little friend is something I can erase from my memory," he called. "I think you look *real* sweet."

"Right," he shot over his shoulder. "Glad I can be your entertainment for the afternoon."

"And I thank you for it. Seriously, I hope you find the owner."

"Me too. If not, I'll bring this little darlin' back to you to take care of. Might help *you* find a date."

Drake's laughter followed him. "Smart aleck," Cooper muttered and rode on.

It hadn't been easy, but Beth finally stumbled to flat land on the other side of the ravine. Feeling undeniably relieved, she stared down at the stream at the base, shuddered and then headed through the trees, limping into the open pasture.

She was muddy, had no telling what tangled in her hair. Her stomach knotted with worry for Tilly and the fear that she might not find her baby goat.

Feeling breathless from all the running around she'd been doing and the panic urging her onward, she walked out of the trees and wanted to kiss the grazing pasture that opened up before her. And she spotted him, the cowboy riding over the rise on his horse. Her gaze caught instantly on the bright spot of red nestled in the crook of his arm.

Relief and a lump of emotion tore through Beth. Her hand went to her throat as her gaze locked with the cowboy's piercing gaze and her breath whooshed out of her as if she'd been kicked in the abdomen. His eyes were an emerald green; they seemed to catch the afternoon sun and drill right into her.

"Have you lost something?" he drawled as she rushed forward.

"You found Tilly." The tiny goat immediately started bleating loudly, struggling in the cowboy's arms trying to get to Beth.

"She found me, actually."

"I'm so relieved. I've been looking for her."

His gaze swept over her and he frowned. "Are you okay? What happened?"

"Ah, I took a roll down the ravine." Beth reached for her baby. "Oh Tilly."

The horse sidestepped away from Beth.

"Whoa." The cowboy's grip tightened on the

reins, tugging them to one side as he halted the horse's movements. "Easy there," he drawled. The horse calmed and stopped moving after a second.

"Sorry." Beth then held her arms out again. "I'll take her."

Instead of handing Tilly over, he climbed from the saddle, still holding the squirming goat. Beth found herself looking up the long, tall length of him. He was a good foot taller than her. She was only five feet two inches, so she calculated his height at about six two. A very nice look at six two with dark hair that curled a touch at the edges. And emerald eyes that caught the sunlight beneath his straw Stetson.

He scowled. "So, you did this to her?" He looked from her to Tilly and then pinned accusing eyes on Beth. "It's ridiculous. There should be a law against it. The question is why?"

"Give me my goat." Beth bristled and took Tilly from his arms.

He rammed hands onto his hips, hips she couldn't help noticing were nicely covered with buckskin chaps. He was something to look at, from the top of his well-worn cowboy hat to the tips of his scuffed cowboy boots. And none of that was anything she needed to be noticing right now.

She frowned at him. "I like to dress her up. You should see how cute she is in her yellow, polka-dotted sundress."

His jaw dropped. "You're kidding' me, right?"

"If I'm lyin', I'm dyin'," she drawled, unable to resist teasing him.

"You're not serious." His eyes narrowed in disbelief.

She nearly rolled with laughter. "Oh, I'm serious all right. She has an adorable pink short set that is too cute to miss." *He* was too cute to miss as he blinked at her as though she were from another planet.

And maybe she was. Her goats had more clothes than she did.

"I don't get it, but I guess I don't have to. I'm Cooper Presley, by the way."

He was one of the Presleys and not one of the

cowboys who worked on the ranch. She had never met them on the few trips that she'd made to the ranch when she'd been younger. But she'd seen them from afar. They'd been impressive in their teen years and if he was an example of how they'd turned out as adults, then they were even more impressive now.

She tried not to let herself be drawn in by his engaging smile.

"And you are?" he drawled when she didn't respond.

"Oh, sorry. I'm Beth Lee, Howard's niece."

"I thought so. I heard through the grapevine that his niece was moving in. When I found your goat, the only place I figured near enough for her to belong to was Howard's place. That's where I was heading when you emerged from the woods. How did you fall? Are you sure you're not hurt?" He studied her intently.

She rubbed Tilly's neck. "I'm fine. I lost my balance on a steep section when a coyote howled and scared me."

"That'd make you jump, all right." He reached out

and she thought he was going to touch her cheek. She stiffened, startled. "A leaf." He plucked it from her hair and held it between two fingers. "It may take a couple of days to brush them all out."

"I guess that's better than a few weeks recovering from a broken bone or two."

"That would have been bad. Especially if no one knew you were out there. Honestly, you don't need to be out here without letting someone know."

Her heart beat erratically as she met his probing gaze. "Yes, you're right. I realize that. I almost called 911 because I didn't know who else to call."

"You can call me. I'll give you my number so you can call me next time you need help."

Her knees melted. "Oh, okay," she said, suddenly breathless. "Thank you. I left my phone in the barn so I'll get it after we get back to my house."

His jaw flexed. "No thanks necessary. Thinking about you laying at the bottom of that ravine with no one knowing you were there isn't something I relish thinking about. Not something I want to worry about again. Call me anytime you need assistance."

She couldn't look away from him. The cowboy was nice. And gorgeous.

Really gorgeous, and when he added a smile at the end of that helpful suggestion, her knees weakened even more.

And that—was not good. She wasn't ready for weak knees and palpitating heartbeats.

CHAPTER TWO

Cooper was trying not to stare but he couldn't help it. His new neighbor was like a bright shiny penny. Her hair sparkled in the sunlight with a mixture of blonde and soft golden browns and despite the leaves sticking out of it at various angles it was pretty. Her eyes were pretty too, large, deep blue and ringed by long fringed lashes. And when she looked at him, they seemed to dig in deep and hold onto him. He could hardly take his eyes off her. But thinking about her laying at the bottom of the ravine out here in the middle of nowhere was unbearable.

She hugged the goat in the red dress and gently rubbed it between the ears. "I'm really glad you were out here to find Tilly. And me."

She had no idea how glad he was. "Me too. If you'd been injured in that fall, you would have—well, I don't want to think about what could have happened."

She looked worried. "I know. Hearing that coyote growling so close was what caused me to fall in the first place." She shuddered. "Anyway, it's all good. You found Tilly, and I made it out alive. And her pretty dress is even still in good shape. That's better than I can say." She placed her hand in her hair and felt around, plucking out several leaves that he'd been tempted to pull from the silky tresses of her hair.

She missed one and he was unable to ignore it. "Here, you missed a couple." He reached for the small leaves and twigs but they were caught up in the tangles. Her big eyes met his, as he had to step close and use both hands to get the leaves out.

"Thank you," she said, softly.

He paused for a moment, tangled up in her eyes

before kicking himself in the pants and finished fishing the leaves from her hair. He stepped back and held the leaves on his open palm. "These did not want to let go." He smiled.

"They're like Velcro. Which makes me curious how she came out so good."

"Her hair isn't as long and thick as yours."

"Oh, that's a good thing. I can only imagine what she'd have looked like."

"Believe me, she was already a shock in her dress. I couldn't believe my eyes when I saw her. My brother Drake couldn't either when I rode back to the herd with her in my arms."

Tilly nudged Beth's cheek, making her laugh, and settled her down and into her arms. "I can't believe how far she came. I don't even know how she got out. I just got moved in and thought the pen was secure. I was working inside the barn for a couple of hours and didn't realize she had gotten out. Then it took me two hours to figure out she was heading across your pasture. Where did you find her?"

"A good way back behind me. I was herding cattle

when she came bounding out of the bushes. I thought it was a kid at first, a real kid because of the dress, and then saw it was a tiny goat."

She smiled. "Okay, full disclosure about her outfit. I was doing a photo shoot earlier and hadn't taken her dress off her yet."

"A what?" Surely, he'd heard her wrong.

Her eyes twinkled. "You heard right. I was doing a photo shoot."

"A what? This encounter is just getting more and more odd." At his words, she laughed, or it could have been his expression considering he knew it was one of complete bewilderment. "But it's certainly not boring." He grinned, curious about this woman.

"Yes, it's a fun project."

He shook his head; he grabbed the saddle horn then slipped a boot into the stirrup and swung into the saddle. He looked down at her. She had a stunned look on her face.

He held his hand down to her. "Give me your

hand and I'll give you a lift home. You can tell me about this goat-modeling gig you've got going as we ride."

She blinked at him, looking like a deer in headlights. "Up there?"

"Yes'um." He pulled a boot from the stirrup. "Grab my hand, hang onto your goat or give her to me, and stick a boot in the stirrup. I'll give you a tug and you'll be sitting behind me in a minute."

"But I have mud on my rump." She bit her lip and continued to stand still.

He chuckled. "Darlin' this horse doesn't care if you're covered in mud."

"But, riding a horse is not one of my super powers. Though I definitely want to learn, I wasn't expecting it to hop on one my first few days on the farm."

"Well, if I may say so myself, you're in luck, because I was born on a horse. So just take my hand, slip your foot into the stirrup, and I'll get you up here behind me and I promise you'll be okay." He held his hand out to her. "Take my hand. I saw you limping.

Besides that, I thought I'd check your fence out when I drop you off."

Cooper wasn't sure whether Beth was going to take his hand or not but he had to admit the thought of her wrapping her arms around him on the ride across the ranch had him hoping she did. He might have called it quits on dating a few days ago, but helping out a woman in distress was not off the table. Besides that, Beth was his neighbor and he wouldn't turn his back on his neighbor.

"I promise I won't bite. And it's a long walk, as you already know, and I'm pretty sure this little gal is hungry."

Her brows knitted at that and she looked down at Tilly. "You're right." She looked back up at him. "I'm being silly." She inhaled deeply as if fortifying her resolve and then slapped her hand in his. "Okay, let's do this."

Her touch sent an electrical charge racing through him as he closed his fingers around hers. "Good for you. Just put your foot in the stirrup and hold onto your goat while I pull you up."

She laughed finally and tightened her hold on Tilly. "I've got my goat and here I come." She clutched his hand as she got her foot in the stirrup and then with a cute grimace she pushed off with her foot while he tugged. One minute she was looking up at him and the next she was slammed up against him with her lips within kissing distance.

"Oh," she breathed, her warm breath feathering over his lips. She froze. His gaze locked with hers. She trembled against him. She was lovely.

Cooper held very still and he contemplated the suddenly enticing situation. "Hi there," he said.

"I...I don't think this is what you meant," she said breathlessly.

"No, but I'm not exactly minding it." And he wasn't. She was pressed against him and when she tried to move, she wobbled. He used his free hand to steady her. "Don't move. I've got you. If you'll just slide your free leg over the hips of Blaze's back, I'll hold you steady while you slide into place behind me."

"Okay," she grunted. Her brows crinkled and her eyes looked serious with concentration as she hiked her leg up and propped it on Blaze's hip.

Cooper couldn't help chuckling. "You're doing good."

"Doing this with only one hand to hold onto something is harder than I thought." She then managed to shift her weight and slide into place. "Whew, that was an experience."

"You did good. Now, settle in and let's get you home. Hold onto me."

His thoughts froze as her arm slid around his waist. He swallowed hard, feeling the warmth of her burning a hole through his shirt.

"I hope you don't mind if I hold on tight."

He patted her arm. "You hold on as tight as you need to. I'll hold on to you."

"Thanks. My hero."

"I'm tryin' real hard to be."

She chuckled. "You're doing a good job."

"Lean against me and you'll be just fine. I don't bite."

She chuckled but seemed to relax as she settled in against him. Tilly voiced her opinion and they both laughed.

"Hang on, sweetie. We'll be home soon," she crooned and he was drawn to her voice.

They rode in silence for a while. They rode across the pasture, through the trees where he knew was the best place to cross the ravine that she had come through.

Finally, he decided he needed to talk to take his mind off the feel of her as she held onto him for dear life. "Your uncle was a good neighbor. We hated to see him leave, but going back to be near his family was the best thing for him."

"He's enjoying being closer to his grandkids but he's really glad I'm here enjoying his farm. I'm glad too. I was so sick of the city. Houston is great, but it was just time for me to leave and follow my dream."

"What's your dream? To take pictures of goats in dresses on a farm?"

She laughed. "No, but I'm doing that because it really helps pay the bills. My dream is to be a farmer."

He was glad he wasn't facing her because he knew his surprise was showing at her words. "A *farmer*?"

"Yes, but I was born in the city, lived all my life in the city and it just seemed out of my reach. Then, Uncle Howard had this great idea for me to move to his place and take over."

The excitement in her words was undeniable. "Well, that's a good plan." *Did she have a plan?*

"You're lucky, having been raised on this beautiful, big ranch."

"I've always counted it as a blessing. But I know a lot of people who can't wait to move out of small towns and to the city."

"For me, it was just the opposite. I was just tied to my job…" Her voice trailed off as Tilly took over the conversation with her loud bleating.

"She's hungry." Beth grunted as he could feel her struggling with the suddenly restless goat.

"We're almost there. I see your barn."

"Good. She wants down."

"Hang on a little longer."

They made it across the last portion of the pasture to the barbed wire fence separating her place from his ranch, with a gate at the road for entrance and exit from the Presley Ranch. He rode up and threw a leg over the horse's neck and hopped to the ground. Then he turned and lifted his arms.

"I'll take Tilly—or both of you." He grinned. Much to his disappointment, Beth handed him the squirming goat.

"Thanks." She then stuck her boot in the stirrup and climbed from the horse. "That was an adventure I hope not to repeat for a while."

He moved to the gate, rolled a combination on the lock and released the chain, then opened the gate to let her pass through. He handed Tilly back over to Beth then tied his horse to the fence before closing the gate. He didn't lock it because he would be using it before heading back home. He headed down the lane toward her house.

She walked beside him. "You want me to give you a ride back to your ranch? I have my truck and Uncle Howard left his trailer here for me."

"Thanks, I may take you up on that. But first let's see if we can find the escape route Tilly found."

"That would be wonderful. Thank you." She

smiled up at him with her crystal-clear, sparkling eyes.

Looking at her, Cooper suddenly felt as though he were falling. He'd just met her, but he had this almost overwhelming urge to pull her into his arms and kiss her as if there were no tomorrow.

Had he learned nothing from his last dating wreck?

He heard what sounded like a goat in distress and looked toward Beth's place the same moment Beth swung around.

"Oh, no. That's Milly." She hurried down her driveway.

Cooper followed. He wasn't sure, but Beth and her goats were starting to look a lot like a disaster in the making.

CHAPTER THREE

Beth raced toward the sound of Milly's distinctive voice, high and shrill as she cried out in distress. Beth had been struggling to act objective after the unbelievable ride back to the house snuggled up against gorgeous Cooper Presley. She could have stayed on that horse, hugging up on him for days— months. Who was she kidding? The man had drawn her like bees to honey and she regretted it when he'd climbed from the horse.

Now, he jogged beside her as she ran toward Milly's wails. Tilly struggled in her arms while crying out for her little buddy.

They found her behind a feed shed near the barn with her little head sticking up out of a hole.

"Oh, Milly," Beth gasped, dropping to her knees. "She's stuck."

Cooper knelt beside her. "She's in some kind of pipe—an old drainage pipe, I think." He gently touched her head then her neck as he bent forward and studied the little black goat. Beth was relieved when Milly quieted down as Cooper checked her out.

"We have to get her out. Can you pull her out?" She shifted Tilly in her arms so that the goat could rub her head against Milly's.

Cooper nodded. "Yes, I can but I need a shovel."

"In the barn."

"Okay, keep her calm and I'll be right back." He stood and immediately Milly started crying out again.

Beth smoothed her head. The goat struggled but she continued to cry out. "Please calm down, Milly." Beth kept her voice calm and was relieved when Cooper came back, carrying the shovel.

Beth scrambled over to the side so he could dig

Milly out.

Cooper would have hurt her if he didn't work carefully to remove the dirt around the pipe.

She was so attracted to her new neighbor and watching his diligent effort to help not just Milly but also Tilly earlier was giving her a serious case of hero worship of the man.

"Do you dress Milly up too?"

"Yes. You think I'm crazy, don't you?"

He concentrated on digging and then his lips twitched. "Nope. But, it's just not my thing."

Beth laughed. "After today, you are my hero, so I'm going to give you an advanced copy of their newest calendar. I'd get them to autograph it but they haven't learned how to hold a pen."

He paused digging. "You don't have to do that, really."

"Oh, but I want to. Tilly and Milly are much more than just pets. They bring joy and peace to a lot of people."

He looked at the little goat. "I'll take your word for it." He moved some dirt then set the shovel aside and knelt beside Milly. She pawed at him with her front hooves.

"Calm down, Milly. Please don't kick the nice cowboy. You're going to want to kiss him when this is over."

She was going to want to kiss him when this was over.

"This could have been really bad and still could be if her shoulders and front legs hadn't caught on the edge. And that shirt thing on her probably helped keep her from going too deep. Okay, here we go." He eased her free.

"You saved her." Beth gasped as the little goat lunged at her, coming free of Cooper's hands while Tilly lunged at Milly.

"Whoa," Cooper said, trying to recapture the goat while she tried to do the same—the goats ended up escaping their grasp while the hunky cowboy hero practically fell on top of her. She fell backward, laughing. Cooper landed tangled with her on the grass.

"Are you okay?" He rose to his elbows to look at her.

"Yes. How about you?" she asked, very aware of his nearness.

A slow smile spread across his face. "I'm doing well, thank you," he drawled.

For a moment, she forgot everything as they stared at each other. His gaze swept over her face and she felt breathless.

"Baaa."

"Baaa."

"Is your goat okay?" he asked, still not moving as they both glanced at the goats.

They were both a few feet away, busily chewing on the brim of Cooper's hat.

Beth gasped. "No. Tilly, no!" Tilly yanked her head up, with the Stetson hanging from her mouth. The hat was bigger than she was. Beth sprang forward and grabbed the goat just as she started to make a run for who-knew-where with the hat in her mouth.

She pulled the animal close and wrestled the hat from the death grip Tilly had on the brim. When Tilly let go, it was with a pretty good-sized chunk of straw hat protruding from her lips.

The hat brim looked awful. Beth looked at Cooper, who hadn't said anything. He did not look happy. Her insides curling up, she handed the hat to him. "I'm so sorry. I'll buy you a new one."

He took the hat, shot a skeptical look at the brim then shoved it onto his head. "No need. It still keeps the sun off." He stood and held a hand down to her.

The instant his hand wrapped around hers, her pulse skittered erratically. He pulled her to her feet. Her reactions to him were overwhelming and she needed to get a grip.

"I don't know how to thank you for what you've done for me today. If you hadn't been here, I don't know what I would have done. I don't even know anyone yet so I guess I would have had to call 911 or something. But you...you were amazing." Unable to stop herself, she leaned forward and hugged him. She barely gave him time to respond before she let her arms drop and she stepped back. Her heart thundered and her cheeks were on fire.

He grinned. "I'm glad I was here. I'm going to fill in that hole and then walk around this place and see if there are any more surprises around that these goats could get into. They are mischievous, that's for certain, and you're going to have a busy life just getting these critters out of trouble."

"I'm afraid you're right. I'm going to put these two mischief makers inside the house then I'll walk around and help you."

"Good. I like teamwork." He smiled warmly.

Beth couldn't look away from him. But she had to. "I'll be right back."

"And I'll be right here."

Oh goodness. She grabbed her goats and got out of there so fast she was amazed she didn't trip and sprawl across the yard. She was not going to let herself get all goo-goo eyed over Cooper Presley. He was now her neighbor and if she'd learned anything over the last year, it was to not fall for a neighbor.

CHAPTER FOUR

Two hours after securing a hole in the goat pen, and making sure Beth had his number in her phone and he had hers in his, Cooper rode back into the ranch grounds, still thinking about his new neighbor. And her goats.

The fact that she actually made money from dressing goats up baffled his mind. But these days, people spent money on all kinds of things he didn't understand, so why not a goat calendar? Of course, he was happy for her and was glad her goat calendar sales were allowing her to start her dream of owning a farm.

He just hoped her farm paid off.

She was pretty but there was something about her willingness to tackle new things that made him keep thinking about her. He wanted to get to know her better. But he was done with dating, at least for now, he reminded himself over and over again. He could be helpful and get to know her better purely out of friendly concern.

Sure, he could. As he rode toward the stables of the large ranch that had been in his family for decades, he wasn't surprised to see trucks and cars everywhere. Tomorrow was Lori Calhoun's wedding to Trip Jensen and they were holding it here on the ranch. Lori was also a neighbor of theirs and a childhood friend. Thinking of Lori proved he could have female neighbors as friends. Problem was, he'd never had any romantic inclinations toward Lori, despite the fact that she was beautiful and they had a lot in common.

He dismounted and shelved thoughts of Beth. He had to help get ready for Lori's wedding. The tent had arrived and they were setting it up. The wedding was going to be a big shindig with a band, and friends from all over were invited. It was his dad's wedding present to Lori; her daddy had passed away this last year and he'd been one of Marcus Presley's best friends. Lori had asked Marcus to walk her down the aisle in place of her dad and Marcus had accepted. He also asked whether he could pay for the wedding as a gift and in honor of his longtime friend. The gesture had brought tears to Lori's eyes as she'd hugged his dad fiercely. Cooper had been touched by the gesture and though he was always proud to call Marcus his dad, he was especially proud that day.

Trip, Lori's fiancé, was Cooper's longtime friend and had asked him to be his best man. Which meant he should have been back sooner to help his buddy out on overseeing everything but he'd gotten sidetracked with a goat in a dress and its pretty owner.

His brothers Vance and Drake were unloading hay from a trailer near the tent.

Drake waved him over. "When you put your horse up, can you come over here and help?"

"Be right there," he called then dismounted at the stable. He quickly unsaddled Blaze and brushed him down before putting him in his stall. His thoughts kept drifting to Beth despite his efforts not to think about her.

"What're the bales of hay for?" he asked when he was standing beside the trailer.

Vance hefted a bale from the trailer. He was the only Presley brother still chasing the rodeo dreams and the rigorous schedule to qualify for the National Finals Rodeo. He was the best roper of the bunch but the more dangerous sport of riding broncs was what he set his NFR dreams on. He'd taken the week off from competing in order to be here for Lori and Trip's wedding.

He dropped the bale beside the tent. "It's extra seating around the edges of the tent. Lori wanted the look of a country wedding and a ranch wedding, and she thought it couldn't happen without bales of hay sitting around. I kind of agree."

Cooper grabbed a bale. "Sounds like Lori. Of course, she wants it as Western as she can get it. She's probably wearing boots with her wedding dress."

Drake grabbed another bale. "I don't know about

that but she and Trip are so happy, they probably would get married in a horse trough. Honestly, those two are so in love I wouldn't be surprised if Dad doesn't start having ideas about us."

"Maybe y'all," Vance said. "I'm not planning to slow down from competing long enough for him to get ideas about me any time soon."

Cooper gave a dry laugh. "I've already said I'm done for right now. I need a break, so Drake, that leaves you, Brice, and Shane."

"Did you know Cooper is calling off dating?" Drake asked Vance.

"No way." Vance halted in the middle of picking up a bale of hay and laughed. "You big flirt, no way you're stopping dating. I'll believe that when I see it. Man, you see a girl and before you know anything about her, you're flirting and asking her out."

Cooper frowned because the truth hurt. "Right." Resolve smoldered in that single word. "Nicole has cured me and made me see the light. If and when I start dating again, it will be with far more discretion."

"I heard down at the diner that TJ Walker found a

new job in another state to get away from her."

"Yep, heard that same thing a little too late." Cooper studied his brothers. "I made it clear to her that we aren't a couple and never were. I just took her out three times and the last time was to tell her I wasn't going to ask her out again."

"So you took her out to break up with her?" Drake asked.

"No, I took her out so not to hurt her feelings or anything."

Vance's brow crinkled. "I see that worked out well for you."

"She wasn't real receptive of me telling her I didn't think we were a good match."

"Obviously," Drake said dryly.

"Hey, I've learned my lesson."

Vance took the last bale of hay from the trailer. "Like I said, I'll believe it when I see it. But did you find the home of the goat in the dress?" He grinned. "Drake told me about that. I couldn't believe it. Sounds like a rodeo clown act."

"True. That is what it sounds like. But nope, turns

out it's a dwarf goat dressed up for a photo shoot for a calendar spread."

His brothers both looked stunned and baffled, and after their teasing about his dating life, he enjoyed a moment of satisfaction humming through him at their expressions.

"It's true. Howard's niece is living at his place now and that's one of the businesses she has going. And apparently her goat calendars do well. I found her out in the pasture looking for Tilly and gave her a ride back to her farm."

"You gave her a ride back?" Vance asked.

"I did. And when we got to her place, another little goat had gotten out and was stuck in a drainage pipe and I had to dig it out."

"Did you flirt with her?" Drake's eyes crinkled at the edges.

"I didn't flirt." *Not technically.*

Both his brothers started to laugh.

Brothers—sometimes they were relentless. "Hey, I didn't," he declared. Despite the fact that he certainly wanted to.

"Is she pretty?" Drake's lips quirked on the edges, as if he were ready to bust out laughing. Or that he knew something Cooper didn't know.

"She's very pretty." It didn't count that he had thought about it but his brothers did not need to know that. "She's as pretty as this pretty lady," he said, as Lori strode toward him.

"Cooper, I've already given all your brothers and your dad a hug." She threw her arms around him. "Thank you so much for all of this. I'm overwhelmed."

"We're just helping out family. You're family, Lori. And so is Trip."

She blinked back emotion. "Thanks. I love you fellas." She swiped at tears.

"Hey, what's wrong?" Cooper exchanged looks of alarm with his brothers.

"I'm a little overemotional today. But also, I have a problem. My photographer just canceled. I don't know where I'm going to find a photographer this late. The rehearsal dinner is going to start in three hours and the wedding is tomorrow. The couple of photographers I know have other plans."

Drake, usually the problem solver, looked thoughtful. "I can barely take pictures with my phone or I'd offer to help. But surely there's somebody who could do it."

Vance shrugged. "Don't look at me. I've had my fair share of pictures taken of me on a bucking bronc but that doesn't mean I can take pictures. Surely you can come up with someone. Maybe a friend who is decent."

Cooper felt bad for his friend and was trying to think of someone who could help her.

"Hold on, I wasn't asking you guys to take pictures, so relax. I just hoped you might know someone. But it will be okay. I'll go make some more calls. Anything will be better than nothing. I had hoped to have some really good ones with a really good camera." She sighed. "I'll just keep looking. Try to figure what I can do. But my bridesmaids will be out later. They're all trying to think of somebody to call but honestly, it's not looking good."

Beth. Suddenly Cooper's brain clicked. If Beth took professional photos of her goats and made calendars out of them that people paid money for, then that meant she was probably a good photographer. "I might know someone," he said, and all eyes turned toward him.

Lori looked hopeful. "Who?"

"Well, I met our new neighbor on the other side of the ranch. And she takes photographs of her goats and sells them. If she can do that, maybe she could take pictures of the wedding."

Lori looked slightly confused. "Goats?"

"Yes, in outfits."

She smiled. "Cool. Sure, if she can make a goat look good then maybe she can make me look good in my wedding dress. I'd be grateful for her help."

Cooper scowled at her. "Even I could make you look good in a wedding dress. The photo could be scratched and out of focus, and you'd look smokin' hot."

Drake and Vance agreed.

"I love you guys. You're really good for a girl's ego. Lana is lucky to have you five for brothers."

"Man, if she were here, she could have taken your

pictures."

"I hate she has the flu."

"Me too. But she's feeling better. Okay, we better do this. Do you have time to come with me to ask her if she can take your pictures?"

Lori smiled, looking relieved. "Yes, I can. And I want to see her goats."

"They're about two feet tall."

"I bet they're adorable. Let's go."

"We'll keep things rolling here," Drake said.

"Thanks." Cooper started toward his truck and wondered whether he should have kept his mouth shut. But this was for Lori and if he could help in any way, then he would.

He couldn't help wondering what kind of situation they would find Beth and her goats in when they arrived.

Beth was walking out of the house, carrying empty packing boxes, when a white truck pulled to a halt behind her truck. She set the boxes on the porch step.

With the afternoon sun behind them, she had to shade her eyes with her hand in order to see who her visitors were as they climbed from the truck. Her stomach tilted when she saw Cooper. When she saw the pretty female with him, she wondered whether it was a girlfriend. *The cowboy was wonderful, so of course he would have a girlfriend.*

And what did it matter to her anyway? She smiled as they approached. "Hi, you're back soon."

He gave that cocky grin that instantly set her insides fluttering in all kinds of chaotic directions inside her chest.

"I brought my friend, Lori, over to meet you. She has a little bit of a problem."

Lori stepped up and smiled. "It's good to have a new woman in the neighborhood. With all these cowboys who live around me, I'm excited to have you here. If you need anything, my ranch is just down the road, past the Presley Ranch."

"It's so nice to meet you, Lori." Beth fought down the unwanted disappointment at realizing Cooper had a girlfriend. Lori seemed nice, so she didn't want these feelings hindering their future friendly relationship. "I'm excited to be here. What kind of problem are you having? Is there some way I can help?"

Lori's smile dipped and she hesitated. "Actually, Cooper told me you are a photographer, or at least you take photos of your goats and do well selling them. At least he said he thought you did. I'm getting married tomorrow and tonight is my rehearsal dinner and my dilemma is that my photographer had a family emergency and has canceled. I can't find anyone and I'm just wondering…is there any way that you could take the job? Cooper said you take professional photographs, so I thought maybe…" She looked pleadingly at Beth.

Cooper put his hand on Lori's shoulder and squeezed gently.

He wasn't only dating—he was getting married. Beth forced herself not to look into Cooper Presley's beautiful eyes. She had been stunned by the news and now, seeing his loving caress of his fiancée's shoulder, gave her a sinking feeling. She'd just met the cowboy, so this was ridiculous. But, if he was about to be married, then end of story; she was not into mooning over another woman's man.

"I'm so sorry about your photographer." She hoped her voice was steady. "I haven't been formally trained as a photographer but I'm good. I have a good eye and I love taking photos, so I would be honored to help you out. If you want to see some photographs of my goats or other pictures I've taken before you decide, I'd be happy to show you. I've never done a wedding, though—never thought about doing a wedding—but you can't have a wedding and not have pictures." She smiled, sincerely hoping that she could help.

Relief washed over Lori's face. "You are a lifesaver. You'll be able to come to the rehearsal dinner to take photos? It's in three hours, at seven. And I would love to see your photographs and your goats. But just because I think they are probably really cute."

"Yes, I can make seven, and I probably need to come a little early to take some shots before people start showing up."

"She's right, Lori." Cooper spoke at last.

"Right. Whenever you want is fine. I'll be dressing there at the main ranch house so me or Cooper will be watching for you and will show you around when you get there."

"I'd be glad to," Cooper said. "You're great for doing this, Beth."

Despite everything she knew, his words of gratitude sent goose bumps pricking up on her arms. "I'm glad I was available. And that you thought to mention me. Well, if you want to see the goats, come inside the house. I have the mischief makers inside their playpen." She turned back and grabbed the screen door and held it open. Instantly, the baby goats began to make noises. She laughed. "They know new suckers are coming that they can con."

"Not me." Cooper huffed. "They've already tried to eat my hat. I've learned my lesson and won't be turning my back on them."

Everyone laughed.

Lori nudged him affectionately. "So that's what happened to your hat."

"Yup. Both the little rascals took bites out of it."

"And I feel really bad about that."

"No need. Like I said, it's ancient and a few calves have already chewed on it."

"He's been needing a new one for ages. I keep telling him to break down and buy one but no, the man gets comfortable with something and it's like pulling teeth to get him to give it up. You just helped him move on sooner. Hopefully, anyway, because it really looks bad."

Beth liked the way Cooper and Lori were comfortable with each other. They knew each other so well. She wanted something like that. She planned on having it the next time she decided to lower her defenses and let another man into her life. Scott had taught her well to be cautious.

It was a lesson she wasn't planning to forget too soon. The fact that Cooper had stirred her interest today just meant that she was still a warm-blooded woman. It did not mean she was jumping back into the dating game. If today taught her anything, it was that she needed to know more about a man before she let herself even think about being attracted to him without knowing anything about his background.

Lori gave a delighted squeal the moment she spotted the goats inside their pen, made from child gates connected together. "They are so cute. I hoped they'd be in their dresses, though."

Beth chuckled. "I don't dress them up in their dresses when they're in the house. Just when I'm trying to get pictures. But wait and I'll grab you a calendar. I owe Cooper one too."

"No, really that's okay." Cooper held up a halting hand. There was no missing his look of complete disbelief that she was really planning to give him a calendar.

The cowboy probably thought she was ridiculous. Fine. She didn't care anyway. She didn't need the cocky, engaged cowboy's approval. Turning away, she strode to the next room, the one that would be her office when she got unpacked. Scanning the boxes, she found the one labeled calendars and after a little shifting around, she cleared her way to it and lifted the lid.

Moments later, she re-entered the living room and

handed the calendar to Lori. "We just got these in and they are going like hot cakes."

Lori smiled and waved the calendar at Cooper. "You should take one because you know you're going to peek at mine every time you come into my office."

"That's a great place for it. I'm not meaning to hurt your feelings, Beth. I just don't have a place for it. I'm in the horse and cattle business and well, the buyers of the Presley livestock aren't going to want to see cute little goats in dresses hanging on my office wall."

She laughed. "I totally understand. But I do like that you called the girls cute. That's enough."

Lori pushed on his arm. "We better get going while you're ahead. Thanks so much, Beth. We'll see you in just a little while. I'm so excited."

"Me too. See you there," Beth called as she watched them leave. Cooper had a smooth but decisive way of walking and he strode straight to the truck and climbed in. Lori's excitement showed as she had jogged ahead of him and was waiting inside the truck as he slid behind the wheel. Lori was thumbing through the calendar but Cooper looked toward the door where Beth stood and lifted a hand in good-bye. Then he swung the truck around and drove out of sight.

Beth sighed then caught herself. "Stop it." And with that, she headed to her messy office to get her camera ready. Then she had to shower and change and get herself to the wedding rehearsal on time. Cooper was getting married; he had been nothing but wonderful to her since she'd met him that morning and Lori was awesome. She was happy for them.

And she planned to document their wedding with the best photographs that she could possibly do.

CHAPTER FIVE

Cooper had showered and changed into fresh jeans, crisp shirt, and his dress boots for the rehearsal dinner. He'd also pulled a newer hat from his hat rack for the occasion. He was checking on getting the drinks iced down when he saw Beth drive into the yard. Drying his hands off, he strode over to meet her. She stepped out of the truck and his steps slowed. She wore a pretty rose sundress and sandals with a slight platform base that gave her a little more height. She looked amazing. It was a heck of a thing when a guy tried not to be interested in women and suddenly he had one who dominated his thoughts completely.

"You should do calendars with you wearing dresses," he said as she pulled her camera bag from the backseat of her truck and closed the door. "I'm glad you came."

She looked confused as she faced him. "I said I was coming. I'm not the type who gives my word and then backs out."

He wasn't exactly sure why he had made such a stupid statement in the first place. "I didn't mean that as a derogatory thing. I was thinking maybe one of your goats might get into a situation and keep you from coming." He grinned but she didn't. Instead, she put a hand on her hip and shot him a look that said she didn't exactly appreciate his teasing.

"I put them in a stall and lined it with the baby gates. They'd have to dig their way out of that stall and I don't think goats are known for their digging skills."

"Right. Anyway, we're really glad you're here. Lori was so worried and you made everything right."

"I'm glad." She sidestepped him as she pulled the camera bag strap to her shoulder.

"Here, I'll carry that for you." He reached for the bag. She hesitated then let him have the bag. "So, how long have you been creating your calendars?"

"For two years."

"But you lived in town. Where did you keep the goats?" he asked, noticing that she glanced around, as if eager to be anywhere but talking to him.

"I had a quarter of an acre backyard. I lived in a duplex. And I had a cute little shed that I used as their house."

"And you never had trouble with them getting out?"

"No, the yard had a chain link fence and had been built to keep a tiny dog inside. So, it worked for the little goats. But, sadly I couldn't keep them as they got older. I had to find homes for them." She looked sad at the thought.

"That had to be hard, since I guess they were your pets and you cared for them."

She nodded. "Exactly. I felt awful. I had used them to make money with and then they were too big so they had to go. I felt like a traitor. But I found a good home for Iris and Lily. But now, I have Milly and Tilly and when they are no longer babies and the focus of my calendars, they will happily be munching on grass and supplying me with new babies to photograph."

"That's great. You know, we have a great county fair. The kids come from all over the county to compete. You might be able to raise goats and sell to kids needing show goats."

Her eyes brightened. "Exactly. That was one of the reasons I moved here. I thought that I could raise goats for goat's milk products and also the county fair. I like the idea of raising show stock. The calendars would be great advertisement for my online business and if I was able to raise champion show stock, they would also advertise that by being babies of champions."

He was impressed. "You've really thought this out. I'm impressed. So, do you know anything about show stock?"

She smiled. "Not much. But I'm a fast learner. And I've bought some really quality goats to build from. They should be arriving soon. They're coming from a well-established seller who does a big business with supplying show stock people who compete in the Houston County Livestock Show and other big shows."

"Good plan. You're not planning a farm over there but an industry. That pretty head of yours has a lot going on inside of it."

She laughed and took a step away from him. "I'm just thinking of everything I can to make my farm support itself." She looked around at the wedding tent and people milling around. "Is Lori around yet? I should be taking shots."

He glanced around. "I don't see her yet. I'll take you over and show you where to set your bag. I'm glad I ran into you in the pasture this morning or Lori would be really upset right now."

"I want to do my very best for her, and for you. I don't think anything happened by chance. I'm a believer that things happen for a reason and Lori needed me today. If you hadn't found Tilly and decided to find out where she belonged, you might not have run into me and I would be home, sad, and so would Lori. You did great. You found out I took pictures and here I am."

"Saving the day," he said.

"No, you saved the day."

"Nope. If you were just a goat farmer, you would not be standing here getting ready to use that camera."

She laughed softly. "That's true."

"I'm really glad you're here." His gaze lingered on her pretty, smiling lips but suddenly she frowned and he met her gaze.

Eyes that had twinkled with laughter were now flared with what looked like anger.

"I really better get busy." She stepped back.

He wasn't sure what had happened but there was a coldness in the air between them suddenly. "Are you okay?"

"Yes, I'm fine. I just better get busy. Time is ticking away on your happy day."

His happy day? That didn't make sense. *What had she meant?*

She suddenly stepped closer to him. "Look, you

should be ashamed of yourself. And to think, I thought you were a nice guy. But you're nothing but a womanizing jerk. Flirting with me on your wedding day—Lori deserves better than this."

He was stunned as realization dawned in him. But before he could clarify Lori came their way.

"Um, hey you two." Lori had her arm linked with Trip's. "Is everything okay?" She looked from him to Beth. "I wanted to introduce you to my fiancé, Trip Jensen."

Cooper met Beth's confused eyes. He bit back a grin and watched the mortification work its way through her, first in the sudden loss of blood rushing from her face and then with the crimson flush creeping upward and across her cheeks.

"This…you are Lori's fiancé?" She stumbled over the words, staring at Trip.

"I am. And she tells me you and Coop have saved the wedding. I can't tell you how grateful I am. I was on the road making a cattle delivery when she called about the photographer's need to cancel. I felt pretty helpless out there on the highway, unable to be here for

Lori when she was upset like that. So, I'm in your debt. And Coop's." He had trapped his arm over Lori's shoulders and tugged her close.

Cooper crossed his arms as Beth swallowed hard and met his gaze. She was really cute when she was pink.

Lori and Cooper were *not* engaged. This was worse than embarrassing and the smug twinkle in Cooper's eyes told her he wasn't going to let her live this down. He had never said he was engaged to Lori. He had just brought Lori out to her house and from their obvious affection for each other, she'd assumed the rest.

"I'm glad to be helping out," she said, weakly. "And now, I better go get some preliminary photos taken of the setup. If you'll excuse me."

She smiled, at least she thought she did, and then she hurried toward the tent. To her dismay, Cooper fell into step beside her.

"You thought I was a real jerk, didn't you?"

"Yes," she hissed, reaching the tent and turning to

him. He still had her camera bag in his hand. She reached for it and he held on, grinning at her.

"Do I look like the kind of guy who would fiddle around on the woman I'm supposed to love?"

She tugged on the strap. "I don't know. I just met you."

He gave her a look that said he did not believe her. "That's all you've got to say?" His lips twitched and looked all too appealing-and now realizing he wasn't engaged...nope, not going there.

She took a deep breath and looked resigned. "I misunderstood. I'm sorry. But you and Lori seemed like a couple when you brought her out to my house today."

His twitching lip went to a full blown sexy grin. "I'm just teasing you. I can see where you might have gotten the wrong idea. Lori and I have been buddies since we were young."

She swallowed hard and tried to ignore the attraction fighting to be set free inside her. "I think it's great how you helped them and I'm sorry I misunderstood."

He let her have the camera bag and crossed his arms. "You do look pretty this evening and I am glad you're here." He repeated some of the things he'd said when he hadn't realized she thought he was an engaged man flirting with another woman.

Not helping. "Thank you. And now, I better get busy. Is this where I can leave my bag?"

"Yes, it'll be fine."

She concentrated on pulling the camera from her bag then hung the strap around her neck. She needed some space to get her thoughts back on track and off of him. "Great. I really better snap some shots. I see cars starting to arrive."

"Go for it. I'll be around if you need me."

Feeling more than humiliated, she walked away from the cowboy and headed toward the tables set up for the meal. She had really misread the situation. She lifted her camera and focused on the table setting and snapped the shot. Then several more of various decorations.

Her mind was focused, though, on one thing. *Cooper Presley was not getting married.*

And no matter how embarrassed she'd been moments ago, the realization that the handsome cowboy didn't belong to another woman made her very happy. And she didn't want to be happy. She didn't need to get tangled up in a romance. Happy was not good.

Not good at all.

CHAPTER SIX

"You must be Howard's niece. I'm Marcus Presley, Cooper's dad."

"Yes, I am." She smiled as she lowered her camera and shook his outstretched hand. She'd taken several photos and now stood to the side, waiting as the pastor and an older woman everyone called Aunt Trudy instructed Lori, Seth, Cooper, and Beth's maid of honor, Shari, a pretty woman about her age, on when to walk in and how fast to walk.

Cooper's dad, in his late fifties, was the epitome of a handsome, successful rancher. He had compelling gray eyes, enhanced by his gray at the temples of his dark hair. It was obvious Cooper hadn't gotten his eyes from his dad. But his build was similar to Marcus's. He had a lean build and was in obvious great shape for a man in his thirties, much less one in his mid-fifties. At least that was what she estimated his age to be. She knew from her uncle that Marcus had suffered a heart attack in the last year, so she was a bit startled to meet a man who looked this healthy and in shape. He looked great, as if he was doing good now and she hoped so.

"Your uncle and I talked before he moved and he was excited about you moving to the farm because you had some really interesting ideas and visions for what you wanted to do with the place. He liked that."

"That's my sweet uncle. He's the best. I'm so grateful he made it possible for me to relocate here. Having a place in the country large enough for me to raise my goats and do my various other projects is just a dream come true." She didn't add that it was at the time she needed the most. She needed to get out of Houston and away from Scott. When her uncle had suggested his place she'd been speechless but grabbed on to the offer as though it were a lifeline to a new life.

Her new life.

Her new beginning.

"I've got plans that I can't wait to implement."

"If we can be of any help to you, let us know. We're right here—we're your neighbors and your friends, so ask for help or anything you need and we'll be there for you."

His offer made her smile because she could tell it was a genuine, very heartfelt offer. "Thank you. Cooper has been very helpful already. And I just really appreciate your kindness and the offer. My uncle said that you were really good people. And he was glad I was going to have such good neighbors."

"High praise coming from Howard. We'll try to live up to it. I better go take care of the other guests now. Enjoy your evening."

She watched him go, feeling a warm glow of gladness. She had good neighbors and that was so very important. She wouldn't ever take that for granted again. Scott had taught her so much she would rather not have learned. But she had learned her lessons. And rather than wallow in self-pity about her last year of unrelenting drama, she would learn from what had happened to her and move forward.

She watched as Lori lined up at the back of the tent. It was time to work. Glancing toward the front, her gaze collided with Cooper's. He stood beside Trip in the traditional position of the best man. A warmth rushed through her and she inhaled sharply.

He was not an engaged man. Voices in her head sang the verse with joy. It took all of her mental effort to tune the verse out. She was not on the market right now. Not yet and not with her neighbor.

That was one of the lessons she'd learned from Scott. Never mix love or romantic inclinations with neighbors if you hoped to remain neighbors in good standing in the future.

Turning away, she focused on Lori and Shari as they prepared to practice their walk up the aisle. It was time to do the job she'd been hired to do and ignore the pull of attraction that could possibly lead to heartache, disappointment and more…if history were to happen to repeat itself, then much more.

As soon as the wedding practice was over, Cooper made a path straight to Beth. She had been all over the place while the preacher went through the wedding procedures and he'd had a hard time concentrating.

Especially when his brothers had made their way over to her and had obviously introduced themselves as she was working. Now, she was surrounded by them.

"The goat rescuer is here," Brice said as he walked up.

"That's me." He scanned his brothers' faces and saw mischief in their eyes. They all could tell he was interested in Beth and were laughing at him because they knew they'd won the bet. He hadn't gone long without flirting with a female. The only problem was, they didn't know that there was something about Beth that compelled him to flirt…or at least to be interested in her. Flirting came naturally when that was the case. "They're mischievous little ladies that did not want to acclimate to their new pen. They wanted to explore the world and it got them in trouble. Almost got Beth in trouble." He still hated thinking about her falling down that ravine.

"What happened?" Drake asked, concern in his words.

"I fell in the ravine when I was searching for Tilly."

"And you were alone?" Vance asked.

She nodded.

"Not a good situation," Brice added before she could say more.

Shane shook his head. "Were you hurt?"

"She has a slight limp," Cooper said.

"It's practically gone. It was nothing. But I learned my lesson. I'll call Cooper next time. Or someone, and let them know I need help. I just didn't realize Tilly would go so far."

She had to endure all of his brothers putting their two cents in on how badly her situation could have turned out and he felt sorry for her. But he had also noticed she'd said she would call him. His brothers had noticed it, too, but he knew they were as concerned as he was. He also knew they could tell that Beth was a really nice girl and he hoped they weren't going to give him a hard time.

"The goat pens are secure now," he interjected in the ongoing conversation. "They won't be getting out any escape holes again but I'm not putting it past them to learn to climb the fence or anything else that's inside."

"Good. I think mischief is what goats are best at," Vance said. "In the rodeo, when they unload the goats for the goat tying event, they're all about trying to get out of the gate. It happened a few times and was a pure mess."

Everyone laughed.

"Do they wear dresses all the time?" Brice asked.

"No," she said with a giggle. "I promise you, I don't get up every morning and play dress up with my goats. I was doing a morning calendar shoot and when I finished, I didn't immediately remove their outfits. I went into the barn and got busy. When I came out, Tilly was missing. I've offered Cooper a calendar but he's refused. If any of you would like one, I'll be happy to give you a complementary one."

All four of his brothers looked conflicted with how to turn down her offer. He grinned. *Served them right for betting he had a dating problem.* Nicole had made him step back and be cautious going forward but he didn't have a problem.

Beth had never been surrounded by so much male good looks in all of her life. Each of Cooper's brothers had a look all their own, each handsome in his own way. How they were all single was a mystery. Trudy, their aunt, had supplied her with that information during the evening. As their aunt, it was easy to see she was hoping to do a little matchmaking.

Vance yanked his cowboy hat off and held it with the fingers of both hands. "I'm sorry, but I have to agree with Cooper on the fact that I can't find a use for a calendar with goats in dresses."

The others quickly agreed.

"What about horses in dresses?" she asked, unable to resist. Their looks of alarm at the idea had her almost dying with laughter but she held it in. "Just kidding. Relax, fellas. Trying to put a dress on a goat is hard enough. I can't imagine putting one on a horse. But Velcro would probably help...Velcro makes anything possible."

Cooper shook his head. "Don't get any ideas. I wouldn't need that calendar on my wall either."

Drake held a resemblance to George Strait in his prime, and his lips lifted into a crooked smile. "You're good," he said. "You almost had us all. You're all right, Beth Lee."

She smiled broadly, liking the oldest brother very much. All of them were great. "I couldn't help myself. And I think you're all right too."

She looked at the Presley brothers and suddenly saw another calendar. No, no way, she put the idea out of her mind. They wouldn't go for a Presley brothers calendar. But goodness, it was a great idea. A get rich quick idea. The thought made her smile.

"I think I see your mind working in double time right there," Cooper said. "Are you thinking about all the different kinds of calendars you could create?"

She was startled that he read her mind. "Well, actually, yes, I was. For some reason, I just realized I could expand my calendar business. There's probably a market for other cute farm animals. Pink pigs, for instance. I need to get some piglets. Calves and colts might be cute—"

"No traumatizing the horses, please." Brice laughed.

"Have you ever been in a pen with pushy calves when you're trying to feed them?" Shane asked. "You'd probably spend more time on the ground getting knocked over than on your feet while you tried to wrangle dresses on calves."

"He's right," Cooper and Drake almost said in unison.

"Maybe you're all right—livestock is not a good idea. But..." She wondered if they would go for posing for one of her calendars. She really liked the idea. Her mind took off with ideas, each one of them holding a goat or a pig dressed in an outfit. Something cute. Her mind exploded with more ideas. If she did a calendar with these guys, that would sell. No doubt about it. Like those hunky fireman calendars, the Cowboys of Ransom Creek would fly off the internet shelves at lightning speed. She was good at marketing and their handsome faces wouldn't need much marketing.

Cooper's eyes narrowed. "I hope you are not thinking of what I think you're thinking. You sure are looking at us five brothers really seriously."

She cringed. *How was he reading her mind like that?* "I don't guess there's a chance of talking you all into a Cowboys of Ransom Creek calendar? I just got this random idea and—" Her words stalled at the look of horror and disbelief etched across the brothers' expressions. They all shook their heads as they took a step back from her. She chuckled. "Okay, cowboys, I was just teasing."

Relief washed over them.

"I better let y'all recover and I'll go take pictures of the dinner." As if she'd given the secret word, they all excused themselves and scattered like buckshot.

Cooper grinned. "That was a cruel joke, but I liked it." He laughed.

She picked up her camera and snapped a shot of him. "I wasn't really kidding."

At his startled expression, she winked and then walked away.

CHAPTER SVEN

Everyone was standing around in clusters after dinner had ended. She'd moved back to the table near the edge of the tent where her camera bag was sitting. Her job was over for the evening and she was preparing to head home. It had been a lovely evening. She'd enjoyed meeting everyone. She had just placed the camera into the bag when Cooper came over to her.

"You nearly scared my brothers half to death earlier."

"I didn't mean to. I thought it was a brilliant idea. Obviously not."

"I'm impressed with your perception and ability to read body language."

"You guys were definitely putting off strong anti-calendar body language. I thought all of you were going to run for the creek." He laughed and her eyes narrowed. "Speaking of which, how did you read my mind on what I was thinking?"

His grin caused a flurry of happy dancing fairies to take flight in her chest.

"I don't know. I just saw something in your eyes. You have very expressive eyes."

His voice had dropped, deep and caressing. She sucked in a breath of shaky air and told herself to look away. But she couldn't.

"Thank you. I'm actually really enjoying this entire experience. I think I got some amazing shots. I can't wait to load them on my computer so I can go through them."

His eyes twinkled. "Maybe you can add wedding photographer to your list of things you're going to do over there on your farm."

"Oh, I don't want to jump to conclusions. The

pictures could be terrible. I won't know until I look them over. But I really am enjoying this and I get the feeling that Ransom Creek might have a shortage of photographers?"

"We do." Aunt Trudy hustled to a stop on her way to somewhere. Trudy had hustled around the rehearsal the entire evening, back and forth from one spot to the other, taking care of details. The older woman was plump, rosy cheeked, and full of life. From what she'd heard, she also ran the local small-town grocery store. "Mary Ellen, bless her heart, is a great photographer but she's getting up there in age and tips the bottle more than she should, making her nowhere near as reliable on good photos as she needs to be. Then Donna, who was supposed to take Lori's wedding photos, has a large family and there always seems to be an emergency with one family member or another. So, short answer, you should set up shop and jump into the pond." That said, she looked at Cooper and then back at Beth. "If I haven't told you already, he's available. They all are. And I might be biased since they're my nephews, but I think they're adorable." She winked and then patted Cooper's cheek and hurried off to wherever she had been heading in the first place.

Beth bit her lips hard to hold back laughter. When he took a step closer, she felt the strong stir of attraction and almost leaned toward him.

They stood face-to-face, closer than they probably should be, staring at each other in a surreal moment. The gun of an engine and then the sound of flying gravel had them both looking toward the parking lot of the ranch. A little red convertible slid to a jerking halt. In the next split second, the door swung open and a voluptuous redhead with never ending legs rose up out of the small car and stalked toward them.

Beth's first thought was that there was an emergency and this woman was coming to give someone bad news. But then she felt Cooper stiffen beside her.

"Not good," he muttered under his breath, drawing her gaze. His expression had gone stony.

Movement over his shoulder drew her attention and her gaze flickered to see Shane and Vance, who had been standing outside the tent talking. They'd both stopped talking and had moved a few steps toward them. Both were watching the advancing female. She looked back at her, too, wondering what was going on. But knowing whatever it was, it wasn't good.

The woman put both hands on her hips. She did not look happy. She glanced toward the wedding tent and started that way. Cooper moved to stand in front of her. And she heard him say her coming to the reception wasn't a good idea.

"Is this the new girlfriend you're trying to drop me for?" she demanded of Cooper then glared at Beth.

"No, Nicole, I don't have a girlfriend. We've been over this already. I didn't drop you. We had just gone out a couple of times. We're not a good match."

Beth didn't think that was the best choice of words but who was she to butt in. Obviously, Nicole didn't like the word choice much herself.

"I'm not a good match but she is? What does she have that I don't?"

Beth looked at Cooper. *What was the story here?* Although she wasn't one for public displays of anger like Nicole, she also had no real idea what Cooper had done. He looked conflicted.

"Come on, Nicole, dating is how you decide if you're compatible enough to keep dating. We went out two times and—"

"We went out three times before you broke my heart."

"I didn't break your heart."

Nicole looked indignant. "I know when I've been dropped and I know when my heart has been broken so don't stand there and tell me what I know and what I don't know."

"What do you want? Clearly, I'm not understanding. I didn't mean to hurt you. But I just didn't think—"

Before he finished talking, Nicole sidestepped Cooper and pushed Beth.

Stunned, Beth stumbled back into the table, knocking her camera case from the table as it overturned. Cooper made a grab for her and caught her arm, keeping her from toppling backward over the table.

Shane and Vance came forward to move between

Beth and Nicole.

"Are you okay?" Cooper asked, appalled at Nicole's actions and concerned for Beth.

"I'm fine," she said, glancing at Nicole.

Cooper glared at the woman he'd just lost all patience for. "That's enough. You need to leave," he demanded.

Ignoring him, Nicole glared at Beth. "He's mine. You back off and go find yourself another man. He just—"

"Enough, Nicole," Cooper demanded. "I've tried real hard to be sympathetic to your feelings but this is going too far."

"You need to leave," Shane said. "This was uncalled for."

"This was Trip and Lori's wedding rehearsal," Vance said. "This is no place for you to be doing this."

"I'm not good enough for you? But she's good enough to date and bring to the rehearsal dinner."

Beth felt terrible about everything she was hearing. *What had gone on between Cooper and Nicole?*

"No, not at all," Cooper said, sounding suddenly tired. He looked as if he had no idea what to do as his gaze locked with Beth's. "She's just here taking photographs. I'm not dating anyone. But, even if I was, I have that right. We had three dates and the third one was so I could tell you I wasn't going to be calling anymore."

Beth cringed, feeling bad for him but for Nicole too.

"You're a real jerk, Cooper Presley. And I thought you were better than that." Nicole spun on her expensive boots and stormed toward her Mercedes.

Everyone watched in silence.

If someone had dropped a toothpick, it could have been heard hitting the dirt. Her car door slamming sounded like the crack of a gunshot and then she revved her engine and tore down the drive.

Cooper yanked his hat off his head and raked a hand through his hair. He looked at his brothers. "What do I do?"

"Nothing," Shane said. "There's nothing you can do. She just has to accept there is nothing between the two of you."

Vance looked as if he was going to add to what Shane said and then shrugged. "Sometimes it just takes time."

"I guess." He turned back to her. "Are you all right? I'm sorry you had to see that and be involved in it. Nicole isn't always like that. Well, I don't think she is."

Beth felt bad for him but she also felt for Nicole. What a terrible situation. Her curiosity had her wondering what in the world had gone on.

After everyone else had left and the rehearsal dinner was officially over, Cooper met the concerned faces of his brothers. He was exasperated and out of his element. He had never had a woman act like Nicole. She'd been driving him crazy for over a month now. She loved to cause scenes; this was the second one. He was trying his hardest to be nice, to be understanding of her obvious hurt feelings, but tonight was the last straw. "I don't know what Nicole wants. But I didn't like her attacking Beth."

Drake crossed his arms. "I didn't like it either and that's not at all. That's the second time she's come on this property and acted like that. When we had our cattle sale a couple months ago and she showed up and threw a fit, I didn't like it. But as for what she wants...that's easy. She wants you. And obviously she's ready to do whatever it takes to get you. But just because someone wants something doesn't mean they always get it. She can't force you to want her."

"True. But, in all of this, there was real hurt in her eyes there for a minute, in the middle of all the dramatics. I put that there and for the life of me don't know what I should have done differently. Never asked her out, yeah, I get that, and believe me, I'm working on it. But I didn't and now she's madder than an uprooted wasp looking for trouble."

"Have you had any communication with her lately that would stir her interest again?"

Shane, Vance, and Brice stared at him with the same question in their eyes.

"No. I'm not going around flirting with her or

egging her on, if that's what you're suggesting. I ran into her at the gas station yesterday, while filling up my truck tank. I tried to be cordial and said hello. I'm not the kind of guy who is just rude to people. She drove up after I was already out of my truck at the pump. We were right across the gas pump from each other so I asked how she was doing."

Four sets of eyes narrowed.

"And I'm guessing she had a conversation with you, since you asked her a question and opened yourself up for one," Brice said.

Cooper felt guilty, looking at his brothers. He hadn't done anything wrong. "All I asked was how she was doing. It just came out. Yeah, she started a conversation. I knew I shouldn't ask." He looked up at the night sky, feeling like a fool.

"And…" Drake drawled, prompting him to finish what he had been saying.

"She told me she had missed me. And I told her right off the bat that I hoped she had a nice day." He tried to minimize the meeting, knowing his brothers were going to go ape over it.

Vance grimaced. "You didn't ask her out, did you?"

Cooper glared at his brother. "No, I did not ask her out. I was trying to get away almost immediately, especially when she told me she missed me."

Brice groaned. "Say it ain't so."

"This is not good," Shane said at the same time.

Drake looked less than pleased, and sighed as if giving up on him.

Cooper glared at them. "Hey, I stopped the gas pump even though it wasn't full and was about to get back in my truck when she launched herself at me." He was not helping his case and his brothers' expressions told him so. He raked a hand through his hair.

"What else?" Drake drawled, exasperation heavy in his words. He groaned. "She was all over me before I could stop her and we almost got tangled up in the gas lines. Come on, stop laughing, Vance. This is not funny. Before I could get her arms unlocked from around my neck, she had a lip lock on me."

"Actually, it is," Vance laughed and tried not to as he slapped a hand over his face. His shoulders were shaking.

"This is getting too ridiculous." Drake scowled, not laughing as he kicked Vance in the shin.

"Tell me about it," Cooper growled, remembering the moment. All four of his brothers' dismayed expressions told him they were probably envisioning the moment themselves. And they all thought he was a fool. He scowled. "Hey, I got myself unlocked, told her once more we were over and had been over. Then I got in my truck and I left."

"You've got a problem." Drake's jaw clenched. "I hope you don't ask anyone else out before knowing something more about her than that she's pretty."

Brice and Shane grimaced but said nothing. Vance had gotten hold of his laughter and kept his mouth shut too.

Cooper's temper spiked. "Give me a break. And if you're not going to offer me advice on how to fix this, then I guess this conversation is done."

"Next time you see her, tell her she's not welcome on the Presley Ranch anymore and that if we have to, we'll call the law. I'm done with scenes." Drake's hard expression clearly showed he was serious. "Dad wasn't happy about it, worrying her actions could sour Lori and Trip's wedding day. He feels a strong obligation toward Ray to not have anything hurt their happy day."

He knew his dad was standing in for his old friend, Lori's father. "I'll tell her." Cooper hoped she would move on. He'd tell her that, too, because it was too much to hope that he wouldn't run into her again. Ransom Creek and the surrounding county was less than ten thousand people, so the likelihood of that happening was slim. But it could be months, maybe. And he didn't like having conflict with a woman, even if she was bringing it on with her own behavior.

Marcus Presley walked up. His gaze drifted to include all of the brothers. "I didn't find that incident to be a good one. I promised to have that wedding for Lori tomorrow and I don't want it being disrupted by something like what happened tonight. If we have to, I'll hire one of the off-duty deputies in town to stand at the entrance gate and keep her out. I don't like the fact that you got this woman acting like this. It bothers me. You're telling me for sure you were a gentleman?"

Cooper stared at his dad. "I'm telling you, I have been, Dad. The fact that you're even asking that question isn't making me any happier."

"I don't like asking it either," Marcus said. "Something has that woman acting irrational, and I am at a loss to figure out what. I am definitely going to ask one of the off-duty deputies to watch the front entrance. She won't be allowed on the property. I'm not taking any chances of her interrupting the wedding."

Cooper rubbed his forehead, a headache forming with the ferocious force of a bull kicking a metal trailer to pieces. "Dad, as much as I hate to say it, I agree with you. Tomorrow is about Lori and Trip, so you need to take precautions so that Nicole doesn't disrupt it."

It was what needed to be done, but it still felt unreal that the precaution had to be taken.

CHAPTER EIGHT

Saturday morning came bright and early for Beth. She rolled out of bed at five a.m. and pulled on her boots while still wearing her cotton gown that hung to her knees. She tugged on a sweatshirt and then headed out to feed Milly and Tilly. She normally fed them a little later in the morning but she wanted to check on them and make sure they were in their pen. They were, thankfully. The niggling worry that they might find another escape route had been in the back of her mind. Finding them standing in the pen with their little faces buried against the fence as they watched her approach was a relief.

"Good morning, girlfriends. How are you two mischief makers today?" Of course, they had started making noise the moment they saw her because they knew her presence meant they were getting food. She poured their pellets into their containers and watched the little gluttons dig in. She laughed, and then headed back to the house. The sun was just starting to rise and she paused on the doorstep to watch the pink and blue hues of dawn brighten into the golden and orange hues of morning. Taking the moment to inhale the fresh air of the countryside, contentment washed through her soul. She was so glad to be here in this special place.

Moments later, she tossed a handful of spinach and a cup of strawberries into the mixer with a couple of scoops of protein shake and mixed it up for her morning breakfast smoothie. She was looking forward to raising her own spinach and strawberries and other fresh produce that she could sell at farmers' markets and other outlets she was going to check into.

Smoothie in hand, she plugged the memory card from her camera into her computer and started to go through the photos she'd taken of the rehearsal dinner the night before. They were good. Maybe not as good as those of a highly skilled photographer but they were still good.

She was relieved that she'd been able to capture these for Lori.

That evening had been fun but challenging. She had been completely distracted by Cooper, despite trying not to be. And when his girlfriend—or ex-girlfriend—had shown up and caused such a scene, Beth had been astounded by the entire encounter. So many questions went through her mind. Questions she had no answers to so far. Cooper and his entire family had been concerned for her but she was fine. However, concerned as they were, they hadn't told her anything other than what she'd learned during the interaction between Nicole and Cooper.

It was none of her business anyway. She'd had her own dating trauma, which was the only thing she could call what she'd been through with Scott. Well, she could call it a nightmare but she had moved out of range of the situation before it went to that phase.

But enough of those thoughts. The only positive she perceived from the scene she'd witnessed last night was that Nicole had been unhappy that Cooper had stopped dating her. That meant she'd been happy while dating him, which was a positive mark on Cooper. And Cooper had seemed genuinely upset that Nicole was hurt by him.

Why would the woman want to create a scene like that?

She paused on a photo of him, smiling at something Lori and Trip said as he stood talking to them in the shot. Yes, Cooper was an amazingly, good-looking guy and had sex appeal oozing off him with his cowboy swagger and crooked grin. Not to mention his dreamboat eyes... *Okay, maybe she didn't need to think about all of that.* The problem about him was the magnetism of the man was effortless on his part. To her, he wasn't the most handsome Presley brother, but he had charisma that just oozed out every pore. And there was no doubt in her mind that women oozed out of every nook and cranny in town as he walked past.

Obviously giving up a man like Cooper must be

hard on a woman, if Nicole's behavior was any indication. Exactly why she had no interest in a man like that. Nope, not only that, he was her neighbor and she already knew that argument, because neighbors were off-limits to personal relationships.

She paused at another photo from the many that she'd taken of him, he was staring across the room straight into the camera lens. Her insides melted with weakness remembering that instant. He'd continued staring at her when she'd lowered the camera.

And she'd almost melted into a puddle then. And now.

Okay, she was so done, so done. It was time to get out of the house and entertain herself with errands and shopping.

A few minutes later, changed into pink ankle-length jeans, a cream-toned top and sandals, she headed to town for her official first visit since becoming a Ransom Creek resident.

And the first place she was going to was Sally Ann's Junk to Treasure shop downtown. She'd been wanting to check out the store from the first day she drove into town. Especially considering she needed a few things for the house and she loved finding older pieces of furniture and redoing it. She was a trash-to-treasure kind of woman and took shabby chic to a whole new level.

In the city, she spent her spare time haunting resale stores and changing out things in her duplex for new items when she found something that caught her attention. She just hadn't had enough space to really let herself go wild. Now, with this three-bedroom rambling farmhouse, she had rooms that needed items. And she didn't plan to do it all at once. She was going to take her time. Like so many of the TV shows, she was a believer in recycling and refreshing. Especially in the home she was now trying to make into her own. Who knew, there was a possibility that she added bed-and-breakfast to her list of things she planned to do in her new life. She felt a little giddy as she parked in the parking space outside the giant building.

She got out and glanced over at the adorable bed-and-breakfast across the street from the Junk to Treasure Shop. Lori had told her that it was also owned by Sally Ann. It was so stinkin' cute with the bright-yellow wooden exterior trimmed in white and window boxes.

From what Lori had told her, there were several people staying at the bed-and-breakfast who were coming to the wedding. She wondered whether Sally Ann might want to carry some of her fresh produce and goat milk products for the B&B. These were the type of questions she would be answering in the next few months as she got her plans ironed out and her garden growing.

She walked up the steps and through the double open doors and she stopped. A sense of anticipation filled her.

An older woman with a long, obviously bleached blonde ponytail greeted her from behind a counter just inside the door. "You've got the look of a woman on the hunt for something special." She nudged her battered straw hat back and smiled. "My name's Sally Ann and you just make yourself at home. Anything I can do to help you, just let me know."

"Thank you. I'm new in town. I've been wanting

to get in here to look at what you have. I have a house in need of furniture and I'm looking for several pieces."

"You can see I have plenty of that."

Beth smiled at the way she waved her hand around to indicate the array of furniture in the store.

"I'm Beth Lee. My uncle lived next to—"

"The Presleys. You've moved in next to Trudy's nephews." Her eyes lit up. "That's a great group of male beauty all in one place. And you're living right there next to them." She made a clicking noise with her tongue. "That's a dream come true if ever I saw one."

It was obvious that no one seemed to be oblivious of the fact that the Presleys were good-looking guys. Or single. Considering they all seemed to be pointing that fact out to her. She got the feeling there was a sense of matchmaking in the air revolving around those cowboys. *Who could blame them?*

Beth slapped a hand to her hip. "Well, they are undeniably good-looking, I'll agree with you there. But, though I love a good love story as much as every female alive, I'm not looking for one myself at the moment. Now, give me some good neighbors and I'm all over that. And I have found out firsthand that they are good neighbors."

Sally Ann laughed. "Cooper rescued your goats. Trudy came by this morning to tell me all about the rehearsal dinner. She told me that Cooper rescued your goats and then you saved the day by agreeing to take pictures. And then you got waylaid by that spoiled Nicole. Now there's one who doesn't know when to give up and move on."

Beth got a lot of information from that statement. One, gossip happened fast. Two, Trudy and Sally Ann were good friends. Three, Nicole was thought of in a universal way by all she'd met so far and spoiled was the single-word descriptor that fit best, it seemed. And four, she liked Sally Ann because she was a straight shooter.

"That's the general impression I got from my encounter with her. But you know what, I'm just interested in furniture. Things I can use in my home office specifically, for today. Do you mind if I look around?"

"I've got something for everything. I'll show you the desks, though you might want to look around and see what strikes your imagination for something else that could be used as a desk. This place is huge and full of all sorts of great treasures." She waved Beth to follow her and wove her way through a maze of eclectic furniture until she reached a section of desks. "I get the idea you're not looking for a regular desk like these. I think I got them from a bank that remodeled. You want something special."

She was right; none of these looked anything like what she was envisioning in her thoughts. "You're right. I'll just wander around and see what I find."

"That's the fun part. Have fun and give me a holler when you find something you want."

She found a perfect piece rather quickly and knew it the moment she saw it. It was a cabinet with several compartments that would be perfect to use in an office. It wasn't a desk but it would be a perfect addition to her space. It was a beautifully aged deep golden-toned yellow. And the price wasn't bad at all.

Sally hustled to see what she'd found the moment

she called her.

"Oh yes. A lot of the stuff right here in this area is from an estate sale I bought a bunch of things from recently. That's one of my favorite pieces. You have a really good eye."

"Thank you. All I know is it will go great in my office."

"Come up to the desk and I'll write up an invoice for you. Do you want my delivery guy to bring it out this afternoon?"

"Could you do that? Today?"

"Sure. He's making deliveries now but when he gets back, I'll have him load it up and bring it out."

"That will be wonderful. Oh, but I may be at the wedding."

"I will be too. I'll just have him put it on the porch, if you can get it inside on your own. Maybe one of those handsome neighbors could help you." She smiled with mischief.

"I'm sure I can figure something out." She could easily ask Cooper or one of the other Presley brothers. They'd offered.

"Sounds great. And I'm getting some more shipments in tomorrow that I recently bought so you can come back next week."

"I'll do that."

"And maybe I'll come out and see your cute goats sometime—if you're having visitors."

"Oh yes, that would be wonderful. And, that reminds me I wanted to ask you if you would like to carry some goat milk products later on after I start making them?"

"Sure. I'd be happy to. And by the way, I hope you don't judge Cooper by the actions of Nicole."

She was thinking about Sally Ann's words as she headed to the grocery store to grab a few things. She had grabbed her peanut butter and bananas and rounded the corner, heading to the register, when she came face-to-face with Nicole.

Immediate recognition showed in the woman's eyes as she glared at Beth.

"You." Disdain dripped from the single word. "Stay away from Cooper. I'm warning you. He's mine."

This woman definitely had a problem and obviously lived in a delusionary world. It was a little bit unsettling.

"I was there taking pictures last night. What is between you and Cooper Presley is none of my business. If you'll excuse me, I need to leave." She moved to sidestep her.

But Nicole grabbed her arm, sinking her long nails into her skin. "You can't just walk off when I'm talking. Stay away from him. And if you don't, you'll be sorry."

Beth was not a confrontational person and this wasn't her fight, so she really, really wasn't comfortable being involved in yet another of Nicole's scenes. And besides that, she had known Cooper Presley for two days, and hadn't even seen him today so she wasn't even sure two days counted yet.

Cooper's Aunt Trudy hustled from the grocery store office to take her spot at the register. Her sympathetic gaze met Beth's and then swung to

Nicole. "Leave her alone, Nicole. And my nephew too."

"I came in here to tell you that I'll be there tonight and if I see you with him, like I said, you'll be sorry."

This woman had problems. Something was just not right about her. And despite not liking confrontations, Beth did not like to be threatened, especially with her arm stinging from the five imprinted fingernail marks that had broken skin. "I told you this is between you and Cooper. There is nothing going on between Cooper and me." The whole situation just got to her. "But, you know what? If there was, it's not any of your business. He has clearly asked you to leave him alone. And this is not the way to win friends, or especially boyfriends."

"She's right, Nicole." Trudy placed Beth's items in a bag and held it out to Beth. "Take these. On the house."

Beth took them, grateful for the escape. "I'll pay you later. Thanks." She took the bag and started toward the exit, more than ready to get back to her farm. She had not left the city to be embroiled in this kind of mess.

"Take her advice, Nicole, and move on. You need to start having a healthy relationship."

"Mind your own business, Trudy."

"This is my business," Trudy said.

Beth was already out the door, headed toward the truck. Nicole trailed her. It was apparent that Nicole enjoyed scenes. Beth had her keys out and punched the unlock button before she reached her truck. She pulled the door open, placed her small bag inside and then climbed into the driver seat. The other woman put herself between the open door and the truck, making it impossible for her to pull it shut. "Move, please," Beth said, determined not to let her have her way by getting involved in a scene.

"He's mine. I knew on our first date that I was going to marry him. And then he broke my heart. I will win him back. I don't need competition."

Beth couldn't believe this. "You need a doctor. Or a hobby. Something. But this is not the way to win a man over. Now, I have to go. Please step back."

To her relief, Nicole did step back and she slammed the door and locked it. She was still glaring at Beth as she drove out of the parking lot.

The last thing she had expected when she moved here was a vindictive ex-girlfriend.

CHAPTER NINE

The wedding went off without a hitch. Cooper hadn't been this relieved about something in a long time. He was just more than thankful that Nicole hadn't shown up. His dad had hired an off-duty officer to man the front entrance. The sheriff was a good friend of theirs and was at the wedding as a guest, so she would have had a hard time causing too much upset. But even a little was more than Lori and Trip deserved on their wedding day.

By the time the reception started, he decided that maybe it was okay to approach Beth. She had been moving around the grounds, doing her job and stealing his attention. She'd been exactly in his line of sight when the preacher asked for the wedding rings and he hadn't heard the question because he'd been distracted by how pretty she looked in her baby-blue dress that hugged her slight curves to perfection.

"Looks like you're doing a good job." He smiled and held out a glass of punch to her. "I notice you haven't taken time to get anything to drink so I thought maybe you might be thirsty." He didn't miss the hesitation in her gaze. It was driving him crazy, her avoiding him.

And she had been avoiding him.

"Thank you. That punch really looks good." She let her camera hang by the strap around her neck and took the cup from him.

Their fingers brushed and he enjoyed the spark of electricity. "So how are your baby goats today?"

"They're as cute as can be. And they did not escape, so I am assuming that you found their escape route and I can now relax. I really didn't sleep well last night worrying whether they might have gone exploring by morning."

"That's good to know I fixed it. I hope you weren't up last night because of what happened at the rehearsal dinner."

"Um, no. Not really. How are you doing today?"

"I'm doing fine. But I'm glad things were quieter tonight."

She grimaced. "Yes, me too. That was a little intense."

"I'm sorry you had to see that yesterday-that you had to be pulled into it like that. I obviously made a mistake somehow. All I know is I don't understand Nicole's behavior." What he did know was he was ready to move on from all things Nicole. He hated she had some type of problem going on but he knew in his heart he hadn't done anything to cause this. He'd stayed up late into the night thinking and going over everything and he had nothing to feel bad about.

Beth bit her lip, looking as if she had something to say. He waited to see whether she would share her thoughts.

"Okay, it's none of my business, but from what

I've seen, there is no amount of bad behavior from one person that is going to make the other person want to date or to continue to date them."

He studied her, thinking... "You sound like you know that from firsthand experience." It was a hunch but something in the sound of her voice told him she was speaking from personal experience.

"Well." She inhaled, as if to gain courage. "To be honest, I've experienced a little harassment of my own, to a certain degree. So, I don't know what has happened between the two of you to make Nicole act the way she's acting, but I know in my situation I just misjudged his character. Anyway, I better get back to work. Pictures to take, you know. Enjoy your evening."

He watched her walk away and had to stuff his hands into the front pockets of his dress jeans to stop himself from reaching for her and asking what had happened to her. To ask her who the jerk was who had hurt her.

His gut burned knowing that someone had harassed her. *Who and why?*

He knew he wanted to hear the whole story. He needed to know she was okay.

Why had she told him that? She hadn't planned to mention the troubles from her past to anyone. She had moved here to forget them. To forget Scott and everything associated with him. So why had she mentioned anything that suggested even the hint that she had had something bad in her past?

She saw the curiosity in Cooper's eyes. The flare of anger. He had not liked knowing someone had been ugly to her. That knowledge had sent her heart thundering and it was still pounding. She hadn't had anyone to stand up for her three months ago. But she had the feeling that Cooper would have stepped in and protected her.

But she had protected herself. Just like she'd always been doing.

She glanced over her shoulder to where Cooper had been standing but he was gone. Disappointed, she turned back just in time to snap the photo of Lori and

Trip cutting the cake. She smiled, watching them feed each other a bite of the buttercream cake.

By the time the music started up and Trip took Lori into his arms, Beth was feeling so overwhelmed watching them. They were so in love. So very in love.

She stood on the edge of the dance floor after all the wedding party dances were over. She had glanced around, trying to find Cooper, but he had disappeared.

"So," Cooper whispered in her ear from behind her. His warm breath caressed her skin and sent a shiver of excitement through her. "I think it's time for the photographer to take a moment to enjoy a dance on this beautiful evening."

She turned toward him, and found herself almost in his arms. "I'm working."

He smiled and took the camera from around her neck. "Not for this dance. Hey, Shane, hold this, please. I'm about to take the beautiful photographer for a spin," he called to his brother, who was standing nearby with a group of females.

"Sure." Shane took it and grinned. "I might try my hand at a few shots of the two of you for the memory book. Lori's going to want to see Beth in the pictures too."

"That's a very good idea, brother." Cooper took Beth's hand in his and led her out onto the dance floor. A slow song was just starting and he twirled her once then pulled her into his arms. "I've been waiting all evening for this dance."

Beth couldn't breathe as she looked up into his spruce-toned green eyes. Eyes that held hers in a mesmerized grasp. His fingers wrapped around hers and squeezed, applying pressure that, though gentle, seemed to burst through her. His masculine scent, a mixture of aftershave and leather, filled her senses as she exhaled and then quickly drew in another, shaky breath.

She swallowed hard. "I've always loved this song," she said, though she didn't have a clue what song was playing.

"I'd love any song that gave me an excuse to hold you in my arms."

"Oh," she gasped, breathlessly. She told herself to get a grip and remember this was her new neighbor and she already knew she was not interested in starting any romantic infatuation with the man for that one single fact. And there were even more reasons than that for why she needed to stay away from handsome, manly—very manly—Cooper Presley. His hand resting lightly on her back pressed her a little closer and he moved them about the dance floor in a swaying waltzing rhythm that only made her ignore the voice of reason chattering desperately in her head.

Cooper sent feelings soaring through her that were more than she'd ever dreamed of; she hadn't even known sensations like this existed. And when his lips curled at the edges, she wanted to kiss the man as if it were the end of time.

"You dance well." He leaned close so the words brushed over her ear like a caress. He was almost a foot taller than her; she wasn't one who'd ever dated a man this much taller than she was, but she was happily changing that where Cooper was concerned.

The song ended too soon, but that was probably a good thing considering she had lost her head while in his arms.

"I better get back to taking the last of the pictures," she said, not sure how she put coherent sentences together considering she felt totally off-center. She felt that way for the rest of the evening.

After his dance with Beth—his amazing dance—Cooper didn't want to dance with anyone else and had gone to stand in the shadows where he could watch her work while at the same time keep a lookout for Nicole, just in case she'd made it past the front gate guard.

Beth had caught his interest and was not letting go. He stood off to the side of the punch bowl that Aunt Trudy and Sally Ann were watching while enjoying the reception.

The ladies came straight to him. Aunt Trudy wore that matter-of-fact look Cooper and all his brothers had come to love from their determined aunt. She'd helped grow them into adulthood with that same kind of determination. Now, he wondered what had put that look on her face and also the twinkle in Sally Ann's blue eyes.

"Ladies," he said in greeting. "Having a good evening?"

"Not as good as you, it seems," Sally Ann said, grinning slyly.

Aunt Trudy poked a finger in his chest. "Cooper Presley, you looked mighty cozy with our newest resident of Ransom Creek."

He hadn't been prepared for this. His gaze dropped to her short finger poking his breast bone. He met Trudy's gaze and hitched his brows in question. "And that would bother you why?"

She crossed her arms and dropped her chin. "Because Nicole thinks you and she are still an item—"

"We were never an item."

"Fine. But nevertheless, Nicole thinks you two are still an item. And she's giving Beth a hard time about it."

He stiffened. "What does that mean?"

Trudy and Sally Ann looked at each other and then back at him.

"You've got a problem, you good-looking hunk of

trouble," Sally Ann drawled.

"What?"

Trudy cocked her head to the side. "Nicole practically attacked that poor girl in town when she'd come into the grocery store to get a few things."

His temper flared at the thought of Nicole attacking Beth again. His aunt kept talking as he tried to hold his temper down.

"Nicole told her you were hers and that she should back off. And then Beth told her that it wasn't any of her business and that Nicole should move on. It was tense but that short, little Beth didn't even look scared. She just turned and walked out to her truck with Nicole following her. I had my finger on the 911 button and was about to call the sheriff, but Beth got in her vehicle and left. Left Nicole standing there, fuming."

His gut clenched. "Thank you for letting me know."

Aunt Trudy stuffed her hands on her hips and glared up at him. "Well, you can't just leave Beth hanging out there as a target for that spoiled, bridezilla wannabe."

"That's right," Sally Ann added. "From what Trudy told me, it was just a miracle that Nicole didn't tackle Beth and yank her hair right out of her pretty head. That can't happen."

He knew that was right. His gaze found Beth taking pictures of several children who had started dancing on the dance floor.

What was Nicole's problem? His dad had suggested getting a restraining order. But he wasn't afraid of Nicole; he just hadn't wanted her to mess up Lori and Trip's wedding. But maybe Beth needed a restraining order.

"I'll take care of it, you two. Thanks for letting me know. Beth is in good hands with guardian angels like you two looking out for her. We can't allow Nicole to be harassing people on the street."

Trudy and Sally Ann nodded, and then Sally Ann elbowed Trudy.

"Tell him."

"Fine." Trudy huffed. "Cooper, you should know something else. You know I'm not one to spread gossip—okay, well, sometimes maybe I do my share of it. But, Darlene—you know, from down at the Roll Up and Dye Salon—you know Darlene hears a lot down there and well, she's a real talker. Cute as a bug but still, a big talker."

"Okay, Aunt Trudy, what did you hear? I know Darlene's a talker." He'd gone to school with Darlene and knew she could talk-and that was the understatement of the year.

"Oh, sorry, here's the scoop. Nicole was in there telling several of the women that she was going to marry you. And I'm beginning to think she thinks it's true."

"She's got good taste, I'll give her that." Sally Ann patted him on the shoulder. "You better figure something out or maybe just run for the hills or she might rope you and drag you down to the sheriff's office to share nuptials."

That made him laugh at the picture of that. "That's not happening. I better go find the sheriff."

CHAPTER TEN

Beth stood on the front porch, staring at the large cabinet and trying to figure out how to get it inside. It was big and heavy, and there was no way she was moving it on her own.

Before the sheriff had shown up in her drive, she'd felt a jolt of excitement when she saw Cooper. She had had him on her mind ever since leaving the wedding reception last night. But seeing the two together sent a shiver through her, wondering whether something bad had happened.

She stepped off the top step, stomach suddenly

churning as she waited for them to walk across the yard. "Hello, Cooper, Sheriff. What brings you two out this afternoon?"

Cooper's eyes met hers. *Their rich, jewel green had her thinking of lazy afternoons curled up together in a hammock on the beaches of the Florida Keys...* She didn't need to be thinking about anything that had to do with romantic anything. She pulled her eyes from his and looked at Sheriff Reb Dawson. She had met him last night. He was a very handsome man, with rugged good looks that had her thinking about climbing mountains and fighting off wild animals. And he was totally male and sexy. The sheriff might stir attraction in women. But she felt absolutely no stir of attraction or anything else for him.

None. Zip. Nada.

However, not the case with the handsome, virile man standing beside the sheriff. He had all her spark plugs sparking and firing on all cylinders.

"Beth, I brought Reb out here because I wanted him to talk to you about getting a restraining order against Nicole."

Beth just stared at him and then at the sheriff; he pulled his Stetson off and held it between both hands. "Excuse me, you want me to do what?"

"Cooper and I both heard about your run-in with Nicole. And everyone is concerned for you."

Beth's temper simmered. *How dare he?* "Well, I'm sorry he had you drive all the way out here for nothing, but I'm not doing that. There is no reason. So, you can stop wasting your valuable time and head back to town."

He hesitated. "Are you sure?"

"No, she's not." Cooper stepped onto the bottom step, making her have to look up even though she was standing two steps up from him. "Nicole almost attacked you in town yesterday. Why didn't you tell me?"

"Sheriff, I'm not filing a restraining order. I don't know what Nicole's problem is but I don't need protection."

"I can't make you do it. But if you do get worried, call me or come in and set it up."

"Thank you, and if I thought I was in danger I

would do it."

Cooper looked positively livid as Sheriff Reb headed back to his SUV and then drove out of the drive.

"Why did you do that?" he demanded. "That was a really bad idea."

"Me? Why did you do that? If I thought I needed protection, then I would have done something about it. I don't need you stepping in and going over my head about things that involve me."

"Because I feel responsible. You shouldn't have to worry about being attacked when you go to town."

He was worried about her. The knowledge softened her anger some. That small voice inside that wished for a hero was feeling good about it. But she just didn't feel right about this. Nicole had problems but Beth didn't get the same warning signals from Nicole that she had gotten from Scott. "I can take care of myself, Cooper. You may be my neighbor but I don't need you trying to take charge of my life." *Been there, done that. And relocated to escape it.*

She could see frustration in Cooper's eyes.

"I don't like you not getting protection but maybe I overreacted. But I feel responsible for you."

"Well, don't. I'm one stubborn female. I might be small but I have a mind of my own and I'm not afraid to use it."

"That's for certain." He grinned.

Mesmerized by him, a warm fuzzy feeling filled Beth. *What was happening here?* "Um, could I get you to help me since you're here?" She was grateful that the thought slipped into her stumbling mind just when she needed it.

"Sure. What do you need?"

"Help moving this into the house." She placed her hand on the cabinet.

"Cool piece of furniture. What exactly is it?" he asked, studying it. He pulled out a drawer then pushed it closed.

She watched as he ran his hand along the dark wood and pulled open another drawer to look inside. *He had nice hands*, she thought, then realized she hadn't answered. "Um, I'm not sure. Maybe it went in an office in years past. Maybe a bank or something with lots of papers that needed separation. I saw it and knew it would look great in my office. It spoke to me."

He cocked his handsome head at her. "Spoke to you. What did it say?" His lips quirked to one side.

She smiled, feeling his teasing like warmth from a heat lamp. "Buy me."

He laughed. "It is pretty awesome. You sure you're going to be able to help me move it? It's kind of big. What if I come by later and bring one of my brothers to help get it inside?"

"Hey, I'm stronger than I look."

His expression told her exactly what he thought about her declaration. "Come on, this thing weighs a ton."

"The delivery guy got it here by himself."

Cooper grinned. "If he moved this by himself, he had a moving dolly. Or he's Superman. And unless Sally Ann changed delivery guys, I can guarantee that he is *not* Superman."

She grimaced. "Oh, right. Why didn't I think about that?" Beth hated her small stature.

"Because," Cooper drawled, reaching out to tug at

a strand of her hair. "You were too busy jumping me for getting Reb out here." His eyes teased her.

"This could be true."

His gaze drifted over her, sending a shiver of delight over her despite his lack of confidence in her.

"I don't know—I wouldn't want you to get hurt."

Frustration seized her. "Don't count me out yet, cowboy."

"I would never do that."

She was standing close to him and her adrenaline hummed happily at his closeness. She wondered how anyone resisted the man. *Poor Nicole. Poor woman must have fallen hard for him, and letting go was taking its toll on her.* Not that she was giving the woman an excuse. She wasn't, but it would be hard to think he was hers and then to know that he was moving on. No, the man had far too much appeal to not fall hard for. She could only imagine how women probably chased after him, not in the weird way that Nicole was doing, but like normal women. She wasn't comfortable with that—sadly felt a little inferior in a situation like that. Didn't like thinking about all the women who had probably competed for his attention.

When he stepped closer, she suddenly wasn't thinking at all.

"Beth," he said, gruffly. "I want you to know I'm glad you moved to Ransom Creek. I'm sorry all this has happened." He lifted his hand as if he was going to touch her; then, instead, he let his hand drop to his side.

He really hated causing her trouble. If he only knew how much trouble he was causing right now by his nearness and his touch to her skin. She swallowed hard. "Stop worrying. I'm a big girl—well, not technically according to a measuring tape, but I am a big girl." She smiled. "Now would you please help me move this thing?"

"Okay, but the minute you look like you're struggling, I'm going to grab a brother."

"Stop, and grab one end of this thing."

"Like I said, I'll be back with reinforcements."

She pushed open the front door. "That is not fair," she said. "Besides, once we get it across the threshold, I have these things that go under the bottom of it that enable it to slide across the floor. And the office is the first room on the right."

"Okay, let's try it. I'll take the end going in first—it'll be heavier. You push."

"Fine." She laughed, knowing there was no way she could budge the cabinet on her own and knowing he was right about where she could be the best help.

A few minutes later, after a little bit of exertion and frustration on her part because she wasn't as much help as she wanted to be, they managed to get the cabinet into the front hallway.

Breathing hard, she was relieved to have made it that far. She leaned her back against the wall and grinned up at him. "We made it. See, I knew we could."

His brows met. "Yes, we did. And we've lived to tell the tale. Where to now?"

She was suddenly very aware of how close he was and how relaxed she was and how much she was enjoying his nearness. She straightened. "I need to get the discs. Like I said, they will make it easier." She grabbed four moving discs from the side table. "Lean it over so I can slip these under the edges."

"Do you buy things you see on infomercials often?"

She let her mouth drop open and glared at him. "I'll have you know that these work."

And in just a few moments, she showed him as they easily pushed the hunk of wooden cabinet across the wooden floors and into the office.

"Well, paint me impressed." He removed the discs from the cabinet when they had it against the wall where she wanted it.

"Told you."

"Yes, you did."

"Thanks. I couldn't have done it without you." They stared at each other and she was not ready for him to leave.

He handed the discs to her and when she reached for them he didn't let go. Instead he held her gaze with eyes that caused butterflies to tumble from her chest to her stomach.

She swallowed. "I guess you have horses or something to go ride," she said, trying for something to relieve the sudden flare of attraction between them.

He let go of the discs and his lips quirked upward. "I always have horses to ride. Didn't you say you wanted riding lessons?"

She wasn't sure she could trust herself taking riding lessons from him. He was definitely hard to resist. "Um, yes, but I have so much to do," she blurted out the truth.

"I do too, but I bet we can both work it in if you really want to learn."

Drats, he was right, she really wanted to learn. And he was offering. She bit her lip and let that sink in and then, despite all the things telling her not to spend time with him, she ignored them. "I would love that then."

"Good. How about tomorrow? Around ten?"

"Oh, so soon? Sure. That would be great."

"Then it's a date." He turned and headed toward the door and she followed, not sure about the date part but pretty sure he hadn't meant it literally.

Once on the porch, he turned back to her. "See you tomorrow. And call if you need anything."

"See you then." She watched him spin on his boots and saunter to his truck. She groaned. *Why was she so attracted to him?* That was about the silliest question in the universe and she knew it.

The real question was how was she going to not let herself fall for the cowboy?

CHAPTER ELEVEN

He had been looking forward to Beth's riding lesson all day long. He'd taken heat from his brothers but he was way past caring by now. He did tell them it was just riding lessons. But not one of them believed him. He didn't believe it himself.

When she walked into the barn, his mood perked up and so did the speed of his heart. She wore her faded jeans, tucked into her boots, and a cotton top with a scooped neck and no sleeves. Her arms were nice, well defined and pale, as if she hadn't spent much time outdoors in the sun. "Hey, you look like you're ready to take a ride." He grinned at her, hooked his boot over the lowest rung of the stall and leaned back against the rough wood as he crossed his arms and enjoyed the view. *She got prettier by the day.*

"I am. I thought about it all night. I've got tons of stuff to do and yet here I am, about to take my first lesson. But I can't help myself. I really want to learn."

"You're going to take to it real quick, I think."

Her blue eyes sparkled. "Do you think so? I should since you're probably the best at what you do."

"Whoa there, little lady, I wouldn't go stretching the truth if I were you. It'll only make my fall that much harder."

"And you're modest, too. I'll add that to the list."

"You do that. But now, let's get down to business. This is Ivey." He indicated the horse with its nose sticking over the stall not too far down the corridor.

Beth stood still. "Is she safe?"

He frowned and let his heel drop from the rung to the ground with a thud. "Now, do you think I'd give you one that wasn't?"

She laughed, looking nervous. "No. I don't know

why I said that." She held her hand out to Ivey and when Ivey nudged her playfully, Beth laughed again in surprise.

"She's hinting for you to pet her."

Beth gently laid her fingertips just above Ivey's nose and then spread her hand out and ever so lightly rubbed the white patch. He had the sudden wish that it was his cheek she was touching so softly. "She likes it. You'll get more confident as we go." He reached for the halter he had hanging over the top of the stall and moved over next to Ivey. "Come over here on this side of the stall and I'll let you help put this on her."

Beth did as he asked and came to stand close at his side. She looked up at him and all he could do was think about kissing her. *This was going to be harder than he'd thought.*

"I'll just watch you put it on her this time. I'm just not comfortable doing it right now."

"Okay, but next time you'll put it on her." He slipped the halter on the horse. "Now for the saddle. I'll do it too."

"Thanks. Even though I'm impressed by how still Ivey is, I'm just not comfortable yet."

"You'll be a pro in a couple of weeks."

She chuckled dryly. "Now don't go getting carried away. If I were you, I'd hold back a judgment like that until after you've seen me in action."

He had pulled the saddle blanket and the saddle from the saddle rack and paused to stare at her. "Do you always have this much lack of faith in yourself?"

She winced. "Sorry. This isn't sounding too positive, is it?"

"Nope. Let's try to be a little more upbeat."

She smiled then nodded. "I'll do that."

He nodded and then placed the blanket on Ivey's back and smoothed it down before lifting the saddle onto it. He reached for the cinch and tightened it up, then checked to make sure everything was in place. "And that's how it's done. Not too much trouble at all. Main thing is to brush her down before to make sure nothing's caught between her and the saddle blanket that could rub a raw spot or be uncomfortable."

"I would see where that wouldn't be a good thing. You're very good at this," she said.

He teased her with a cocky smile. "Well, I'd hope so. I'm here to impress."

She laughed. "You've done that from the moment I met you."

Immediately her cheeks tinged pink. And he smiled wide. "I have, have I?"

"You don't have to look so cocky. But yes, you have."

They stared at each other, him wanting to touch her so bad he could barely keep his hand tightened on the reins. And she looking as if she were torn between wishing she'd kept her mouth shut and wishing he'd take a step closer and kiss her. But he figured that last part was just wishful thinking on his part.

He cleared his throat. "Good to know. We better head out to the round pen." He started to walk, leading the horse. Beth fell into step beside him. Her arm brushed his for a moment, sending electric pulses through him. She moved a little to the left, away from him as if she'd felt it too. He wondered...

He also wondered how in the world he was going to behave himself and just teach her to ride.

Once they were out in the round pen, Cooper told her to climb up into the saddle. Beth had been fighting her attraction to the sexy cowboy from the moment she'd walked into the stable and spotted him standing in a beam of sunlight, looking like every woman's dream of a cowboy. Long and lanky with shoulders that were wide and strong and filled out his button-down shirt like a dream. The sleeves were rolled halfway up his arms, revealing strong forearms that she could well imagine wrapped around her, holding her close. His jeans rode his hips as though they'd been hand stitched for him. And then he'd started teasing her in that way he had and she'd found it almost impossible to concentrate on anything but him.

Now she stared up at him and then back at the horse. Though it was standing perfectly still, patiently waiting on her to stick her boot in the stirrup and then swing up into the saddle, Beth frowned. "How?"

He grinned and then bent over next to her, laced his fingers together and held them about knee high. "Step here and then the stirrup."

Was he kidding? "Isn't there a box or something?"

"No, ma'am. Just put that little boot of yours right here in my hands and I'll help you up." He looked up at her. "Or I could pick you up and pitch you up there."

She stuck a boot in his hands and then reached up as high as she could and grabbed the saddle horn. With his help, she stepped into the other stirrup and then swung her leg over and was into the saddle within seconds. Her heart pounded. He placed a hand on the saddle next to her knee and looked up at her. "That wasn't so bad, was it?"

"A workout for a short girl but from up here, everything looks great. And I can actually look down at you for the first time."

He smiled. "So that's a big deal?"

"Oh yes." She got the urge to lean down and kiss him. The flash of longing blindsided her. Everything about Cooper drew her to him. She felt as if she were on the verge of something important. *Could she take a chance on letting what was between them be anything but a friendship?* They were going to be neighbors for a very long time and from the looks of what was going on between him and Nicole, being on the outside, looking in after things didn't work out with him, might be hard. Nicole was certainly not handling it well. Not that she would handle it like Nicole but still, something told Beth that if she were in Nicole's shoes, she wouldn't like watching him date someone else. She yanked her wandering thoughts up tight. She wasn't dating the cowboy.

"So now what?" she asked with way too much enthusiasm as she tried to put her thoughts back on track and get this lesson started.

"Well, your hands." He gave her a slow smile and her hand tightened on the saddle horn as he took her free hand in his. His touch sent longing rampaging through her. Her pulse ricocheted through her.

"Hold the reins like this," he showed her how to hold the reins.

She really found it hard to concentrate on what he

was doing, but she tried. "Like this?"

He met her gaze and heat simmered between them. Was he struggling too?

"Your grip is a little tight." He stroked her hands, teasing her stiff fingers to loosen a touch. "That's better."

His touch sent shivers of awareness through her.

"Good," she said, trying not to think about his touch.

"You're doing fine." He stepped back, putting much needed distance between them and she was grateful.

"Now nudge her with your knee. Just a light squeeze is all it takes to get her started on a walk. You're safe here in this round pen; just walk around. I'm right here if you need anything. And then we'll move on, one step at a time. That's the way—you're doing good."

She got hold of her runaway hormones and got her head on learning to ride. Soon he had her maneuvering the horse with basic skills and she was feeling slightly more confident. Of course, she knew that Cooper had given her a very calm horse. Ivey was not the name of a wild bronc.

Even still, Cooper stayed right beside her until he knew she was more confident. Then he stepped out a little bit farther into the center of the ring. He stood with his hands on his hips—*his very nice hips*—and watched her, turning slowly in a circle as she and Ivey made the rounds. She liked knowing he was there.

He worked with her for about an hour, giving her pointers and a couple of times lightly touching her knee. But for the most part, he stayed in the center of the round pen and gave his instructions from a distance. She felt safe with him and with Ivey.

The horse was noticeably used to having riders on her back and this helped Beth build up confidence with her.

"Now let's take her to a lope. Just nudge her with the heel and go with the flow. She knows what to do."

"I was just getting comfortable. And now you want me to make her run."

"Lope. There's a difference." He chuckled. "Trust me. Give her another nudge."

Trusting him and trying to think positive, she nudged the horse like he told her. Almost instantly, Ivey reacted and set up into a quicker pace. The loping wasn't as smooth as the walking and sent her to bouncing in the saddle. *She was going to be so sore.*

"Am I s-supposed to be m-moving up and down like this?"

"You'll get used to the rhythm in a minute. Relax, move with her and it'll smooth out."

"I h-hope so. I'm going to c-crack a molar here in a m-minute."

He chuckled. "I doubt it."

She was bouncing all over. And he was grinning like a schoolboy. She reminded herself that tomorrow she should wear a sports bra—one that would keep her from being so bouncy when she rode.

"Just relax."

She sighed and tried; she had stiffened up so. But at his encouragement, she relaxed her shoulders and tried to not be so stiff. And then something happened and suddenly things smoothed out some and she was moving with the horse. She laughed. "Oh, this is much better. I can't believe I'm doing it."

"Just got to have a little faith. And listen to your instructor."

"Right. I'll try to remember that for future reference."

"That's a great idea," he said, the teasing heavy in his words. "Now pull up and let's get you down from there. That's enough for the first day. Do you want help getting down?"

"I'm thinking positive and I believe I can get out of the saddle by myself, thank you very much," she said brightly. She pulled her leg over the back of the horse and then eased down while holding onto the seat of the saddle. It looked so easy when everyone else did it. But, by the time her boot touched the ground, she had left her right foot in the stirrup and now found herself stretched awkwardly. She pulled herself upward so she could yank her boot out of the stirrup but she couldn't get the right leverage. So, there she hung, one boot crammed in the stirrup, one with the tippy toe touching the dirt and her arms growing tired, clinging to the edge of the saddle. She glanced over her shoulder to find Cooper silently chuckling.

"Oh you." She giggled, unable not to. "This is not funny."

"Oh, but it is. Believe me."

"What do I do?"

He crossed his arms and tapped his chin with one forefinger. "Well, let me see."

She was losing her death grip on the saddle and could see herself falling backward with one boot still stuck in the stirrup. "Would you help me and quit making fun of me," she half laughed and demanded at the same time.

"See, I knew you would figure it out on your own." His smile was as bright as high beams on a black night. "And I'm not making fun of you. I've just never seen quite that kind of dismount in all my cowboy'n days."

"You are not funny. Help, please."

His hands were around her waist in a split second and he lifted her so that her boot slipped right out of the stirrup. And then he set her on the ground. Her back was against his chest and his hands were still on her waist. Her heart pounded as he leaned his head close to her ear.

"You're all safe."

His breath sent warmth fanning out over her skin. After all the fighting off the overwhelming attraction swarming around them all afternoon this was too much. She could feel his chest pressed against her shoulders. She had the undeniable urge to turn around, put her arms around his neck, draw his lips to hers and kiss him. *What would he think of her if she did that?*

She didn't do it. Instead, she turned with the intention of using her brain and getting out of there. But she found herself between him and the ever-present Ivey. The horse was not one to run away easily.

Temptation crashed all around her. "Thank you," she managed to say, though her mouth suddenly felt as if she'd eaten all the dirt in the round pen.

And then he lowered his head and brushed his lips to hers.

CHAPTER TWELVE

What was he doing? He was kissing her before he realized what he was doing. It was impossible not to. He barely knew her and yet he knew her.

It was a feeling he was not used to. And yet he planned to adjust as quickly as possible.

Her soft lips moved with his. She filled his senses, pulled longing so strong from him that he couldn't think. and when her arms went around his neck, his tightened around her. He'd never felt the emotions now rushing through him.

Ivey snickered. The sound brought him to his senses. Or partly. He opened his eyes and took in the beauty of her, with her dark lashes resting against her translucent skin. He pulled back, not wanting to lose the feel of her lips against his. He wanted more but he didn't want to run her off either. The shocked look on her face told him that she had not been prepared for his kiss.

"Sorry," he murmured, feeling the beat of her heart against his ribs. He threaded his fingers through her sun-kissed hair. When she lifted her face to his as he kissed her again, brushing his lips across hers and fighting the need to crush her to him and hold on to her was huge. His senses spun as he forced himself to pull away. "I suppose I should apologize for that but," he said, huskily, "I would be lying."

Her lips twitched with mirth. "Well, at least you're honest." She looked about and then stepped out of his arms, easily ducking around him so she was no longer between him and Ivey. "Thanks for the lesson but I better go. I've got a ton of things to do today."

She backed toward the gate of the round pen and

he wanted to pull her back.

"You did good today. Want to ride again on Wednesday?" He wanted to ask her whether she wanted to ride tomorrow but he had to carry some bulls to a ranch in Bastrop.

"Sure." She bumped into the fence, blushed, and bit her bottom lip. "But, no kissing."

He crossed his arms. "What if I like kissing?" He was teasing her but the words were clearly unexpected. Confusion colored her face and then she laughed and he smiled at the sound of it.

"You're dangerous, Cooper Presley, and I'm not looking for dangerous. No matter how good you kiss."

He grinned. "You think I kiss good?"

Wide eyes met his. "No. I mean, yes, you do. But I'm here only as your neighbor. You're my neighbor. And that's the way it needs to stay." She turned, fumbled with the latch on the gate, then met his gaze as she locked it back up and then headed to her truck.

He was still standing in the middle of the round pen with his hands on his hips. Ivey nickered again. *Neighbors. What in tarnation did him being her neighbor have to do with not being able to kiss her? Or date her?*

As far as he was concerned, not one dadgum thing.

She was losing it. Beth had worked on touchups of Lori's wedding photos late into the night and the next morning. They were going to be home from their honeymoon in three days and she wanted to have these ready for her to view. She had had to force herself not to linger over photos of Cooper. But the truth was, every time he was in a shot, she felt a tickle of excitement and awareness course through her. And she relived his kisses that had taken her breath away and sent her world spinning.

She sighed, propping her elbow on the table, and rested her cheek against her knuckles as she took a moment to stare at him talking with his brothers. Five gorgeous men decked out in well-fitting jeans, Western dress shirts, and Stetsons. *Gorgeous.* But she only had eyes for Cooper.

She didn't need to have eyes for any of her neighbors.

Her phone rang and she didn't recognize the number. She picked it up. "Hello," she said, waiting. There was no answer, so after a moment, thinking it was one of those telemarketing calls that don't connect, she disconnected and went back to mooning over Cooper.

She had a crush on the man.

Even though she shouldn't. She thought of Scott. He'd sent her an email earlier that day. Saying he'd missed her and wanted a chance to make things right. The idea sent a sourness to her stomach. When she'd left Houston, she'd needed the distance that it put between them. She'd hoped the distance would discourage him from trying to have contact with her.

As well as the restraining order she'd filed against him.

She hadn't said anything to Cooper or the sheriff about already having experience with restraining orders. She had felt violated by having to have one against her ex-boyfriend/neighbor and knew exactly what kind of bad behavior deserved filing one. Nicole hadn't crossed that line with her. She wasn't afraid of the woman. She had been afraid of Scott in the end.

Just because he had her email didn't mean he'd followed her two hundred miles across Texas to start harassing her again. And having received one hang-up call didn't need to send her running to the cops either.

So, how had her thoughts gone from thinking good thoughts about Cooper to the pits of her angry, mixed-up past? The hang-up call hadn't helped. It had been a tactic Scott had used in Houston to harass her and try to scare her. She'd changed her number to an unlisted number and hadn't given it to anyone from her past other than very close friends and family who knew the situation. They would not have given it out.

Enough of this. It was time to work in the garden.

She had come here to get away from the likes of Scott the Jerk.

And if he thought she was going to email him back or send him her number, then he was sadly mistaken.

She was just walking outside when a truck pulled

in and she saw goats. Excitement filled her. They had arrived. They were one more step toward putting her in business.

Hurrying down the steps, she waved at the young man as he rolled his window down. "Are you Beth Lee?"

"Yes, and you've got my goats." She was grinning from ear to ear, she was quite sure.

"Yes'm, I do. Where do you want them?"

She pointed toward the pen.

He gave her a nod. "I'd appreciate it if you'd open that gate all the way so the gate will be out of my way."

"Sure can." She hurried to do as he asked then watched as he pulled the truck around and backed the trailer up to the opening. From their smaller pen, Milly and Tilly came to watch, letting their curiosity be known with loud yelling.

"Okay, girls, you have new neighbors but between you two and them, it's going to be way too loud if y'all keep this ruckus up."

She knew after everyone got acclimated the

loudness would calm but goodness, it was a bit much at the moment.

"They're kind of loud but they'll calm down." The driver joined her at the back of the trailer. He opened the trailer gate and a couple of nanny goats jumped from the trailer and raced to check out the pen. Two others, both pregnant, munched on straw and took their time but finally followed the other two into the pen.

"That's it. If you'll sign this slip, I'll get out of your hair."

She took the pad he held out, signed it, and handed it back to him and then, with a grin, he headed out. She closed the gate immediately after the trailer pulled away from the opening and was thankful the four goats were on the far side of the pen. Hopefully, they were used to pens and not the type of goats that were always trying to figure out how to escape.

CHAPTER THIRTEEN

The next day, Cooper parked his truck behind Beth's and laughed at what he saw. Beth was trying to manhandle the old garden tiller while her dwarf goats jumped and raced around inside their pen. The woman and her goats made him chuckle. Today they did not have outfits on, unless you counted the little hats each one of them wore. One had on a pink sock hat, one had on a red one with hearts all over it. Climbing out of his truck, he walked toward them. Four adult goats stood with their paws on the fence, watching Beth wrestle the tiller. She'd said she had some adult goats coming so he wasn't surprised to see them. Two of them were pregnant. No doubt about it; she was going to have babies soon.

The woman was going to have her hands full.

The tiller was making such a racket that she hadn't heard him drive up.

Tilly saw him first and let out a loud yell. She bounced over to him, springing on all fours as if she were wearing springs on her feet. Goats really did move in weird ways, bouncing on all fours this way and that way like springs gone bad. He laughed at their antics and reached into the pen to pet them.

He had to admit they were cute. But not as cute as Beth.

She was hunched over the tiller and hadn't noticed he'd walked up behind her. He touched her shoulder. She screamed and threw herself around to face him.

"You scared me," she accused while holding her hand over her heart.

He winced. "Sorry, I called your name but you didn't hear. I didn't think it would scare you that much."

She slapped him lightly on the arm. "Well, you did. What are you doing?"

"Being bad, evidently." He tried to look contrite. "Honestly, I'm sorry. I should have walked around in front so you could see me. The kids saw me and so did your new nannies."

"It's okay. I'm just jumpy today—and I don't mean that way." She pointed at her jumping baby goats.

"Still, I should be punished, so how about I take that over for you? It looks like it's hard work." Her frown didn't surprise him and he was expecting her to tell him she could do it herself.

"It's supposed to be easy to use. The guy I bought it from said it ran like a dream and churned up dirt like it was running through water. Fat chance that was true. I was just going to whip out a little section before I came over for my riding lesson." She laughed. "Are we still on for riding lessons this afternoon or are you stopping by to cancel?"

"We're still on. I finished helping relocate a pasture full of cattle this morning and thought I'd see if you wanted to grab some lunch in town. Instead, how about letting me give it a go? But first…" He brushed a patch of dirt from her cheek. "Looks like you had a dirt fight."

She went still at his touch and he wanted to do a fist pump in the air.

"I had to get a big clod of dirt out of the blades. I guess I brushed my hand on my face afterward. Thanks."

"Anytime. My pleasure."

She blushed pleasantly and he forced himself not to look at her lips but instead to focus on the tiller, the culprit responsible for giving her a hard time. "Stand back and watch me wrangle this little filly into control."

She laughed. "There goes that cocky side of you. Hang on, because she could throw you over her shoulder and plow right over you."

He shot her a look of horror. "I can't believe you even suggested that. This ain't this cowboy's first rodeo."

She continued to smile. "That's what I'm counting

on. I was just bringing you down a notch."

"Gee, thanks. Watch and be amazed."

Her laughter tickled his insides as he took the vibrating handles of the tiller and got it into motion. The tiller was like holding an airplane motor revved up at full speed. "This is ridiculous," he shouted over his shoulder, his voice shaking as though he were talking through a spinning fan wheel.

"Put some weight behind it. And from back here, you're giving Elvis a run for his money on shaking your lower half. There is definitely a whole lot of shaking going on."

He chuckled. "I'll have to do my Elvis impersonation after I turn this thing off. But right now I've got a challenge to win and a beast to tame."

"Fine with me. I'm rooting you on. Go, Elvis, go."

Two hours after Cooper showed up and saved the day, Beth found herself sitting across from him at the Goodnight Diner for a late lunch before they went back to the ranch for her afternoon lesson. He had insisted he take her to lunch and had blackmailed her with the work he'd done for her.

Gert Goodnight, the owner, was a skinny lady who moved about the diner like a bullet. She was a one-woman show, carrying trays and yelling orders to the cook. But even as busy as she was, she had a pleasant, no-nonsense manner about her. One that probably came from years of being busy and pleasant at the same time. The woman could probably juggle while carrying five plates of food and taking an order at the same time. Beth couldn't take her eyes off the show. Then she noticed others were watching her and Cooper.

"People are staring." She leaned forward so hopefully only he heard her words.

"Get used to it. This is a small town."

She found herself looking around, expecting Nicole to jump out at any moment.

After they gave their order to the waitress, his aunt Trudy and Sally Ann came in. They hustled over the moment Trudy spotted them.

"This is a wonderful sight to see." She beamed

from Cooper to Beth.

Cooper rose and gave each of the older women a hug. "Good to see you two. The Flatbottoms having their weekly meeting of the minds?"

"I'll flatten your bottom, young man." Trudy laughed and swatted him on the backside.

Cooper chuckled and then sat back down in the booth.

"You two making a date of it, I see." Sally Ann looked happily at them. "Good for you."

Beth's worry was coming to life. "No. I mean, we came for lunch is all. Cooper was helping me till up my garden."

"Helping out around the farm? That's a good sign, when a man digs in and helps out. He's a keeper." She winked at Beth.

"Definitely a keeper," Trudy echoed. "All of my boys are." She frowned. "You haven't had any more trouble out of Nicole, have you?"

Beth didn't want to talk about the woman who would probably cause trouble if she saw her with Cooper. "No, but I haven't been to town much."

"Don't let her scare you off," Trudy warned. "She's all talk." She smiled at Cooper. "He's just such a great catch, he drives the women wild."

Beth chuckled.

"That is for certain," Sally Ann agreed. "If I were younger, I'd be chasing him."

"Okay, you two. Don't you have a meeting? Your fellow Flatbottoms are waiting."

"You're asking for trouble, young man." Trudy beamed. It was obvious that this was a running bit of humor between them.

"Hey, did a man call you about your piece of furniture you bought from me? He was just in the shop, looking for something similar and I told him I'd had something but sold it. He wanted your address so he'd come try to get a look at it and make you a deal on it, so he said. I don't give out addresses but I did give him your number. He might make you an offer."

"I don't want to sell it. I love it."

"That's one of the reasons I didn't tell him your name or give him your address. I didn't want him showing up at your property so I just gave him your number."

"Thank you."

"Now, back to eating, you two. But really, Beth, he really is a keeper." Trudy patted Cooper on the shoulder, looking delighted.

"I love you too, Aunt Trudy. You, too, Sally Ann." Cooper grinned as they moved to a booth in the back, where two other older ladies were waiting on them.

After they left, Gert brought their burgers.

"Enjoy. That right there is a Presley burger," she said to Beth. "Best beef in the state."

"Thanks, Gert. Are you shorthanded?"

"You are a smart cowboy too. I'm impressed. Yes, I am shorthanded. My waitress eloped with her boyfriend to get married. I hope I find a new waitress soon. These old legs aren't what they used to be."

"I'm very impressed," Beth said.

"Flattery will get you a job. You want one?"

Beth held her hands up. "Oh noo, ma'am. You would be as unimpressed by me as I am impressed by you."

Gert sighed. "Got to learn some time. If you change your mind, I've got an apron back there."

After she'd headed off to reload, Cooper cocked his head to the side. "I hope you forgive my aunt and her friend. They mean well. Aunt Trudy just suddenly seems more interested in my love life than normal. But she means no harm."

Beth picked up her burger. "She's sweet and obviously loves you and your brothers. She's been so nice to me. And so has Sally Ann. I'm curious—why do you call them the Flatbottoms? It's a little odd-sounding."

His eyes twinkled. "My uncle used to call the ladies that just to get their hackles up. They meet here for lunch a lot and discuss everything from world peace to knitting. He teased Trudy that her bottom was flattening out from all that sitting. Eventually the men down at the feed store got to calling them the Flatbottoms whenever they were talking about the group of ladies. It stuck."

She had taken a bite of her burger and had to finish it before she could say anything. And also not choke. "Funny story. So now, at least I'll know who they're talking about when I hear the name."

He nodded and took a bite. They ate for a few minutes and then he set his burger down. "If you get a call from this guy Sally Ann gave your number to, are you going to sell him the cabinet if he offers you a good price?"

"No. Well, I guess if he offered me a really good price, it would be foolish not to consider it. I'm not really attached to it yet. And maybe I could find something similar later on. But I don't know." She thought about it for minute. "I might."

"If he calls and you need me to be there when he shows up, I'm available anytime."

"I'll take precautions."

"Call me, okay? A man wanting to come to your house to buy a piece of furniture that's already been sold just sounds fishy to me."

She took a bite of her burger to keep from saying something she would regret. She could take care of herself, but then, with Scott she hadn't really done a very good job of that. "Okay, I'll call you. It does sound a little suspicious."

The door opened and Beth bit her tongue. "Ow," she hissed. Her tongue throbbed as she met Nicole's glare. Cooper had his back to the door and had no idea his worst nightmare had just walked inside.

"Did you bite your tongue? I hate when that happens," Cooper said, oblivious that Nicole was crossing their way.

"Nicole," she whispered.

Cooper groaned and turned just as she reached the table. On the way across the diner, the redheaded beauty snatched someone's water off their table. The moment Cooper looked at her, she poured it over his head.

CHAPTER FOURTEEN

"Why am I not good enough for you?" Nicole demanded, hurt shining in her eyes.

Cooper stood, water dripping from him. He rubbed his jaw, something wasn't right about this situation. Clamping down on his temper, he let the water roll off him and looked into Nicole's eyes. They flashed with anger and there was that hurt there, too.

"Can we talk outside?" he asked, exasperation sounding in his words despite his attempt to hide it. He didn't like drama and that was all he'd been having since he'd made the mistake of asking her out.

"No, I have nothing more to say to you. We're through. Done. And I don't know why I dated you in the first place." She jabbed a finger in his chest—he really hated that. "You're not good enough for me. Neither was TJ."

Cooper leaned forward, trying to hold down his voice, knowing everyone in the diner was listening and watching them. "Then why are you badgering me like this? And harassing my friends?"

She glared at him. "Because you deserve it."

Okay, that did it. "Nicole, I don't deserve this," he said firmly. "And neither does Beth. Just stop. If I'd done something wrong, I wouldn't blame you but I didn't do anything wrong. You're doing yourself a disservice here." *What else was he supposed to do?*

Beth rose from the table. "Nicole, is there something I can do to help you?"

Nicole's angry expression had turned slightly confused as he'd spoken and now her gaze darted to Beth. "No, you've done enough already."

Gert had set her armload of plates down and now came toward them.

Nicole glared at the older woman. "You don't have to come throw me out. I'm leaving." And then she spun and ran out of the diner.

Instantly, talk ensued through the restaurant.

Gert looked at them. "I heard she was causing trouble but this is out of hand. Something isn't right. First, she drove that TJ out of town and now she's doing this to you. I don't get it."

Trudy and Sally Ann came to stand beside them.

"You handled that real well, Cooper." Sally Ann patted him on the shoulder. "Not sure how else you could have handled it unless you'd lost your temper and I was real proud of you for your control."

"Me too," Trudy added. "We're going to go try to find Nicole and talk to her. Maybe we can find out what is really going on."

Cooper looked at the three older ladies, appreciating them. "Thanks. She might need someone. Is she out there at that big house all alone? Isn't her dad on an extended business trip or something?"

Gert frowned. "I guess you could call it that. He took his latest lady friend."

"Sounds about right." Cooper was ready to leave. He'd lost his appetite and felt as if they stayed in the diner, they'd get questions and opinions galore on how to handle his predicament. He wasn't wanting the attention and right now he had all the help he wanted.

Beth watched Cooper talking to Gert and felt a deep sympathy for him. He probably wouldn't like knowing she felt sympathy for him but she did. He was clueless as to why Nicole was acting this way and it bothered him deeply. She had a feeling Cooper Presley was used to having everything under control. And he did not have Nicole under control.

"Did you get enough to eat?" he asked her.

"Yes. If you're ready to leave, I am too." She could tell he was not going to eat anything more and she wasn't either, even though they'd both only taken a few bites of their burgers. Sally Ann and Trudy left to see whether they could find Nicole, and she and Cooper left after he pulled some bills from his billfold and laid them on the table for the food. If she'd thought everyone was watching her when she'd sat down in the diner, she was certain they watched them leave.

Nicole had made sure of that.

When they arrived at the ranch, his brothers and several others she recognized from the wedding and rehearsal dinner as cowboys who worked on the ranch were all gathered up at the arena. Vance was in the middle of the pen, on a horse that was extremely frisky.

Everyone greeted them as they walked up but were distracted, as she was, by what Vance was doing with the horse. It was not happy about having a rider on its back.

"Vance rides broncs on the rodeo circuit. Made the NFR two years in a row and won it last year. He's good with stubborn green broke rides that need straightening up."

She looked up at Cooper. "Okay, so almost everything you just said is Greek to me. What is the NFR? And what does green broke mean?"

He chuckled and sent a zing of attraction through

her. He placed an arm around her shoulder and pointed to the horse. She liked the feel of his arm loosely draped over her shoulder. "It's okay, easy things not to know if you're not from a ranch or paying attention to rodeo. NFR is National Finals Rodeo—happens in Las Vegas at the end of the year."

"Oh, right. I knew that."

He grinned. "And green broke means a horse like that. We get horses that were not gentled up before they had a saddle tossed on their back and ridden rough. They're not always reliable. They can get moody and jumpy. And sometimes just downright ornery. We retrain them when we can. Vance likes to take on the most stubborn and work with them."

"This one is just plain mean," Shane said from where he stood closest to them. "He tossed Rico this morning after you left, Coop, and then he tried to stomp him. Drake had to ride his horse between them in order to keep the horse off Rico. Vance is working with him before he heads back out tonight for a rodeo in Abilene tomorrow night."

"Don't worry, I'm not putting you on a green

broke horse," Cooper said. "Since they're using the pen, how about we go for a ride on the ranch?"

"Am I ready for that?"

He dropped his arm and looped his thumb over his belt. "You're ready. Ivey is very well mannered, so you'll be fine."

Getting out in the open sounded great. "I would love that, then."

"How are your kids doing?" Drake turned from the fence as they were heading toward the stable.

"They're good. I got my new nanny goats earlier today. I'm looking forward to the new babies they're going to have soon."

He looked bemused. "You're going to have your hands full."

"I like it though."

"Sounds like it. Have fun out there." He then turned back to watch Vance as the horse he was on started bucking as though he were possessed.

Cooper had the horses saddled in a few minutes and helped her get in the saddle. She was still a little sore from their first riding lesson and though she was getting better at getting her foot in the stirrup and pulling herself up onto the saddle, it was nice having him assist her.

She tried not to admit that, but it was true and she knew it. Maybe it was because of all that had happened so far today—the email from Scott reminding her of the ordeal she'd lived through, and then the trouble at the diner—but she felt close to Cooper and she felt for him.

"Thanks for coming out here to ride with me," he said after they were riding across the pasture. "I needed this."

She was holding onto the saddle horn and the reins at the same time as she tried to adjust to riding. He was riding beside her and could easily lean over and grab the reins if something went wrong. She felt safe but just hadn't gotten comfortable with the whole process. Still, she liked the idea of being out in the pasture and riding on the ranch. "I needed it too. But it's no wonder you needed it. That was intense back at the diner."

He nodded and stared out ahead of them, as if

deep in thought. "Hopefully Aunt Trudy and Sally Ann can help her move on. But I'm thinking something deeper is going on with her."

"I agree. Life is complicated," she said, breathing in the fresh air and suddenly being so very grateful for being here in this wide-open space. She glanced at Cooper and admitted that being here with him was nice too.

After a few moments of riding and just enjoying the ride, he spoke. "What happened to you? You hinted that you'd experienced something similar to Nicole back in Houston."

There was really no reason not to tell Cooper. Despite the fact that she really hadn't planned to share what happened to her with anyone. She'd planned to start a new life here and not think about the few months when she'd been afraid.

"It's kind of a long story."

"I have all afternoon. Unless you'd rather not talk about it. But I'd really like to know."

"I'll share it with you. I lived in a duplex with a nice yard and a nice older woman as my neighbor.

Then she passed away suddenly and I got a new neighbor about two months later. A man. Scott was a restaurant manager and appeared to be a nice guy. He was handsome and friendly. He would come out when he was home and visit with me when I was in the backyard with my goats. He asked me out one day and I went. We had a nice dinner and a nice evening."

She remembered how normal he'd seemed during that time. She glanced at Cooper, who was listening quietly. "He seemed normal. We started going out a couple of times a week and then it just seemed natural on the evenings when he wasn't at the restaurant, he'd join me for whatever I had fixed for dinner. But then, he started asking me what I had done during the day. Digging for the details and almost drilling me about why I had gone on this errand during lunch or stopped off at that place after work. At first, I dismissed it as interest. But then it started seeming like the truth of what it really was: he wanted to know exactly where I was every moment of my day and he wanted a say in where and what I did. I called him on it. Told him I might be dating him but that I didn't have to have permission from him to go and do what I pleased. It made him angry."

"Did he hit you?"

"No, he apologized. Told me he was sorry and didn't want to upset me. But after that, I started pulling back. But he was living right there beside me and I had unwittingly tangled myself up with him. It wasn't that simple to detangle from a relationship when you were both living right beside each other. He would show up for dinner and I just didn't want to be rude. I see now I should have called it off and put firm boundaries in place. But I didn't. And the truth is that might not have worked either. It began to seem like everywhere I went, I was running into him. And then the questioning started again. And he got really angry when I told him it was none of his business what I did during the day."

"I'm glad you did."

She gave him a tight smile. "I told him then that I wasn't dating him anymore and that I thought it would be best if he stopped coming by for dinner. He didn't like that at all and he ignored me. The very next day, he came to the door and knocked and when I didn't go to open the door, he pounded and pounded. And he came to the back door and did the same thing. I felt trapped."

"Did you go to the cops?"

"Not until he tried to break down my door and started calling me all times of the day and night. He wouldn't listen to me. He caught me in the backyard one evening after I had ignored him all day. And he grabbed me. When he abruptly let me go, I fell down. And he loomed over me and for the first time, I thought he might hurt me. That's when I got the restraining order."

Cooper scowled at her. "But you wouldn't set one up for Nicole."

"I'm not afraid of Nicole. I became afraid of Scott. He was too controlling."

Cooper exhaled a deep breath. "I get it. He didn't hurt you?"

"No, not physically. But he did some significant harm to my self-esteem. I ended up leaving and moving here. He got really weird by following me and, like I mentioned, he was calling me at all hours of the day and night. It was as if he were obsessed with me. One day he came to the accounting firm where I worked and he threw a fit. I can't lie—it terrified me. Thankfully my boss was there and called the cops. He wasn't held long. But I knew there was no way I could stay living there so I took my kids and found a hotel room."

"You were able to take the goats to a hotel?"

She smiled. "I told them I had two small dogs in the carriers and booked a room with an outside entrance. Then I called my uncle and told my cousin what was going on. She immediately told Uncle Howard and within a week, I had managed to get moved here."

He had stopped riding. "That just happened right before you got here?"

She had stopped riding too and nodded. "I have to admit that I wasn't expecting to get involved in a stalking situation right after I arrived. Not that I'm sure Nicole is categorized as stalking but still, it's not fun."

He looked concerned. "No, what's going on with Nicole hasn't escalated to that kind of harassment. But

I'm sorry for having drawn you into it. I mean, I never thought about Nicole doing something like she did when she pushed you at the rehearsal and then bothering you in town. Is that jerk still bothering you?" He changed the subject back to Scott.

She thought about the email and the dropped call. "I got a new number and had it unlisted and he doesn't know where I moved. Though, he had heard me talk about my uncle's farm. There is the possibility that he might figure it out. But there are two hundred miles between us, so I think that's enough space to keep him away. It's very inconvenient."

They started riding again and she studied the beauty of the ranch. West Texas was a beautiful area, with all of its oak trees spread out over pastures that were still green in March. Later, she knew traditionally that when July—or August for certain—arrived, that these beautiful green grasslands would be dry and pale from lack of water. But the beauty would still remain. Here on this ranch, she could see hills in the distance and she already knew there were deep ravines cutting through portions of it.

"I think this ranch is beautiful," she said, filling the quietness with the truth.

He looked pleased, though he didn't smile. "I do too but then, I'm pretty partial to it. My grandfather and grandmother settled here over a hundred years ago. We're planning to keep it in the family for at least another hundred. More hopefully, but who knows what the future holds."

"That's really nice. My parents own a small place about a hundred miles from Houston. I love it there too."

"Why didn't you go there to settle?"

Her mother and dad had tried to talk her into it and she loved them with all her heart, but... "Well, I like my independence, for one. I love my parents and might have gotten a place near them but, at the time, I was looking to get away from Houston quickly and Uncle Howard was wanting to do something with his farm so I moved here. He's financing the deal and was happy as can be that it's still going to be in the family. Besides that, Scott knew exactly where my parents lived, and it's such a small place and not that far from

Houston that he could have found me easily."

Visibly angry, Cooper stopped his horse. "I'd like to see him show up here and try to bother you. If you don't have my number on your quick dial, then put it there."

They had stopped at the edge of a clearing that was full of grazing mama cows and baby calves everywhere. Cooper crossed his wrist over his saddle horn and studied the cattle. She loved the way he looked, sitting there like that. She couldn't help staring and wondered whether he'd ever had his photo taken like that: on horseback, looking across the land that he loved. The set of his jaw told the story of how angry he was.

"It's going to be fine." She felt bad that he had his own problems going on and he was so angry about what had happened in her past. "You don't need to worry about me."

He stared at her but didn't say anything. And then he was out of his saddle so quick she was stunned. But when he reached up and scooped her from Ivey's back, Beth gasped and her heart thundered harder than a herd of bulls. "What are you doing?"

He held her in his arms, one under her knees and the other cradling her back. "I will worry about you. And this jerk better not make the mistake of following you." He said the words firmly yet there was a tenderness in the way he held her.

"Cooper, have I told you since I met you that I think you're wonderful?" Telling him how she felt about him felt right in that moment.

"I think you're pretty wonderful yourself." He kissed her then, holding her in his strong arms. Her hands went to his chest and curled in the material of his shirt. As he deepened the kiss, she melted into him. She'd never felt the kind of emotions that swept her up and carried her away as these that overwhelmed her when Cooper kissed her. She couldn't think straight as his lips worked magic over her own. But it was more than that; something about being in his arms felt right to her. And that was a feeling she'd not only never felt before but not really ever thought she would ever feel.

She kissed him back, lifting her hands to cup his face between them, to feel the afternoon stubble on his jaw as her fingers moved into his short hair. She was floating on a cloud of bliss here in his arms. When he pulled away, she was breathless.

"I don't want to scare you." He looked at her with eyes so lush and green that for a moment she got lost in their depths as if she were stumbling around lost in a rain forest...or the ravine separating her place from his. "But you fill me with feelings I've never felt before. And I will worry about you. I can't not worry about you."

She blinked, his words registering through her thoughts of being lost in his eyes. *He had feelings for her that might be as strong as the feelings she was experiencing about him.*

"I think you should know." He set her on her feet. "I've never been one who thought about serious relationships. I date when I'm interested but never for very long. That's one thing about Nicole—she started talking about marriage on the second date. I'd...kissed her once. Sorry, not exactly the conversation to expect after we've just shared what I consider an amazing kiss. But, that kiss has me thinking, that where you're concerned, I'm in the same position that Nicole seems to be in where I'm concerned and…your ex too. Don't worry, I'm not going to stalk you." His lips lifted in a smile. "But I'm overwhelmed with you. I would be really sad if this didn't move into something serious. I'm really botching this."

She stared at him, at his expression of baffled bewilderment. He was adorable in his bafflement. Her heart twisted as butterflies fluttered in her stomach. She knew what he was trying to say because she felt the same. "No, you're not. Because of what I've experienced with Scott, I had no intentions of starting to date. Especially a neighbor. But…" She smiled softly. "There's this amazing cowboy whom I can't stop thinking about."

He smiled and looped his arms around her. "It's completely understandable why you'd feel that way. About not wanting to date a neighbor."

"True. Scott is a weird piece of work. But, understand this, I'm not doing to you what Nicole is doing to you—I'm not talking marriage. I'm talking about wanting to get to know you better. And then seeing where we go from there."

His gaze never left hers. "Are you sure? You should know I'm thinking serious thoughts about you."

She smiled. "Wonderful." And then she placed her arms around his neck, drew his head down to hers and kissed him. For a very long time.

CHAPTER FIFTEEN

When they arrived back at her house, it was nearly five. She and Cooper had shared a wonderful afternoon and had not only opened up to each other about their recent dating problems, they'd talked about the feelings that each of them felt about the other. It was so not planned on her part, these strong feelings that she felt toward Cooper. He made her smile, feel safe, and she just enjoyed being around him. But something about him just spoke to her, that what she was feeling for him was special. And when they kissed, she saw them walking down the church aisle as husband and wife. She'd never had that thought about any man.

But she didn't tell him what she suspected the future held for them. Nicole may have had the same images in her head and voicing them on their second date had sent him running. Of course, she liked to think she and Nicole were nothing alike. If Cooper told her right now that he didn't think they were going to be right for each other and he didn't want to date her, then she would accept it. Yes, she would hate it, but it took two people all in to make a relationship work. One person could love the other with all their might but that wouldn't make the other one feel any differently unless they were already feeling it.

Nothing would have ever made her fall in love with Scott. Not once she got past the getting to know the real him part and knew there was no future for them. But, what she experienced the first time she met Cooper was different from her reaction to anyone, ever, in her past. It was as if he spoke to her on a higher level.

He walked her to the door. Across the yard, the

goats stood on their back feet and watched them, calling out.

She laughed. "It's never quiet around my place."

"I hear that." He grinned as he waited for her to unlock her back door.

When she went to put her key into the lock, she saw the door was not pulled closed all the way. "I must have forgotten to pull the door shut all the way." She pushed it open as she smiled up at him. "I had going to lunch with you on my mind."

Cooper frowned. His gaze looked past her into her kitchen. She followed his gaze and gasped. Her kitchen had been trashed. Eggs had been taken from her refrigerator and thrown at her kitchen cabinets. Dishes were pulled from the cabinets and lay broken on the floor, and food items from her pantry had been ripped open and poured or tossed everywhere. It was awful.

"Who would do this?" she asked, her voice barely above a whisper.

"Not someone who likes you." Cooper had moved to stand between her and the open doorway. He already had his phone out. "Reb, hey, we have a break-in out here at Beth Lee's place…yeah, good." He pocketed his phone. "Sheriff's on his way."

The hot heat of anger had her trying to walk around Cooper into her house. Drove her forward.

"Whoa there." He grabbed her arms and held her back. "Not a good idea. Let's wait for Reb. We don't want to disturb anything in there. Let Reb look around and then give us the okay."

"Fine," she gritted through stiff lips. "I can't believe this. Who?"

"Let's look around out here and see if we see anything out of place. I'd say footprints but it's been dry. Still, maybe we'll see something."

She spun and stomped from the steps. She'd already lived through Scott's attempts at disrupting her life and to know the small town of Ransom Creek had vandals lurking around didn't make her feel very good about her decision to relocate here.

She glanced around the yard and saw nothing out of the ordinary. Her pulse pounded in her temple and her mouth was dry. Cooper strode toward the edge of the house and studied the ground near the flower bed.

He moved on, around the side of the house and out of her sight. His expression had been stern. She followed him and found him kneeling at the flower bed.

"Did you find something?"

"No." He stood. "I thought the ground was disturbed here but it's nothing."

The sound of sirens could be heard and they both turned to see the sheriff's SUV pull into her drive. He cut the sound and got out and strode toward them.

"Sorry about this," he said to Beth. "You've had one lousy welcome to our community with Nicole's bad behavior and now this."

She searched for a way to respond to that. He spoke the truth. "I just don't get it," she ended up saying.

"I understand that. Don't let this color your opinion about our community. There are a lot of wonderful people but, as with all communities, there's going to be some bad. But we'll do everything we can to find out who did this."

She sighed. "So it seems."

"They entered through the back door," Cooper

said.

"Let's go take a look," Reb said and Cooper led the way back around the side of the house.

She followed and waited for him to enter and then Cooper. Finally, she was allowed inside and her stomach churned with anxiety as she took in the disaster again.

Reb was silent as he looked at the mess himself. Then he walked to the other room and stopped. "Have you seen this?"

"No, what? We didn't enter the house." She passed Cooper and stepped into the living room and gasped. The furniture had been turned over and the curtains ripped off the windows. Photos had been knocked from the wall and the glass had been broken. And what looked like the contents of what had been a full syrup bottle had been emptied all over the furniture. She knew it was syrup because the now clear, empty bottle lay on the floor. Along with the clear, empty bottle of ketchup. Along with what she could only assume was a now empty bottle of mustard.

Her knees went weak at the terrible mess that had

been made in this room. Tears stung her eyes. Cooper put his arm around her, giving her the support she needed. She gripped his arm.

"Are you okay?"

Cooper's gentle question drew her to look up at him. She gained some semblance of her balance back looking into his serious but worried eyes. "If whoever did this wanted to make a real mess...they certainly did it up good."

"It can be fixed. We'll help."

She just looked around, feeling more numb by the minute.

"Cooper, take her outside for some fresh air. I'm going to gather some samples—"

"I'm fine. Shaky and upset but I'm not going to fall apart, if that's what you're worried about. Ask me whatever you need to ask me."

Reb looked steadily at her, as if gauging the truth of her words. "Okay then. Do you have any idea who might have done this?"

She crossed her arms, not wanting to admit that someone might have actually targeted her for this. But at the moment, there was only one very obvious person who disliked her enough to trash her place. She looked from Reb to Cooper. "Do I have to say the obvious? I just moved here, and if this was done by someone who doesn't like me, then you both know that would be only one person. Nicole."

Cooper watched Reb leave Beth's place about forty minutes after he'd arrived. Reb was on his way to question Nicole and though no evidence had shown up so far pointing to her, she was the only suspect. Guilt rode on his shoulders as he turned to find his dad and his brothers watching him.

"This isn't your fault," Marcus said. "Though I know you don't believe that."

"Dad, there is no reason to pacify me. If Nicole did this, and it doesn't look good for her after the way she's been acting, then it is my fault and y'all know it."

"I know I'm not going to change your mind about that, but right now, Reb has to handle it. And if you want to feel guilty, then I can't stop you."

"Nope, you can't. I need to get inside and help Beth. She's pretty shaken up but determined to get as much cleaned up tonight as possible."

Drake stepped up. "We're here to help. Lead the way."

"That's right," Shane said. "From what I saw in there, it's going to take all of us."

The sound of cars pulling into the drive had their attention. The goats that had quieted down some started their noisemaking again as all of them watched several cars and trucks come to a stop. Sally Ann climbed out of her old red truck and Aunt Trudy climbed from her car. Darlene from the hair salon and Gert were all getting out of their cars. They pulled pails and mops and one of them had a huge package of paper towels as they walked toward them.

"Well." Sally Ann paused to look at them. "You boys going to just stand there gawking or are y'all going to show us where we're needed?"

Marcus reached for the two pails she was holding

in one hand. "I should have known you ladies would come charging out here like the cavalry."

"Thanks." Cooper reached for the bag of cleaning supplies his aunt carried. "Beth needs to see how good this community is and you ladies are just what she needs."

He led the way into the house. Beth stood at a kitchen cabinet, scrubbing at the egg slime that was now drying on the wooden door. She looked as if she'd been crying but there were no tears on her face now. Gasps sounded behind him but he was watching the startled surprise flow over Beth's face as she watched the room behind him fill up with people.

"Help has arrived." He smiled. He could feel guilty all he wanted but that wasn't helping her right now. Some light flickered into her eyes and she let the rag drop.

"Hon, we heard what happened and we've come to help." Aunt Trudy put her arms around Beth and gave her a hug. "Don't you worry, it's going to be okay."

"I don't know what to say," Beth said, tears glistening in her pretty eyes.

"No need to say anything. We're going to get this mess cleaned up as good as new." Sally Ann frowned at the mess. "This kind of behavior won't be tolerated. Come on, folks, let's get busy."

"That's right," Gert said, still wearing her apron that she wore at the diner. She had looked around the doorframe into the other room and turned back to them with a look of disgust. "That's a cryin' shame in there. We're going to need an upholstery cleaner. Anyone got one?"

When everyone shook their head. Darlene spoke up. "I'll call my mom and have her run by the store and run it by."

"That would be so nice of her."

"She won't mind at all."

For the next two hours, everyone worked in unison to sweep, scrape, wipe, and vacuum. Her office, or what she'd started decorating as her office, had been trashed also. The large cabinet had been pushed over and had crashed to the floor, destroying a chair it was so heavy. He and Shane lifted it back to a standing position but it was damaged in the fall, having hit so hard. He hated that because it was the first thing she'd bought to represent her new move.

"This thing is heavy," Shane said, as they were lifting it up.

"Tell me about it. I moved it in here with only Beth pushing on one end."

Shane scratched his jaw. "You were really wanting to impress her, doing that."

His brother was teasing him but it was the truth. He wanted very much to impress Beth. As much as he hated what had happened and as guilty as he felt for his part in drawing attention to her with Nicole, he kept thinking about their afternoon. Beth was easy to talk to, and fun to be with and had his attention from the first moment she'd come out of the woods looking for her goat. There was just something elusive about her that had connected to him.

"Shane, I have to say, as weird as Nicole has been

acting, something like this never crossed my mind. Her other actions never crossed my mind."

"Mine either."

"I'm going to go call Reb. He might be finished questioning her."

"I'll finish up in here."

Cooper went out the front door, where it was quiet. He punched the number to Reb. He was relieved when he answered.

"What did you find out?" He didn't waste time with pleasantries.

"I'll be honest with you, Cooper—keep this close. She acted truly surprised when I confronted her. She understands she's a suspect, or the suspect, because of her actions. I'm a pretty good judge of character and she seemed worried. I've told her she better keep away from you and Beth because she can't afford anything else to point at her."

"It doesn't make sense. None of it does."

"I hear you. I'm heading to my office to check out a few things on the computer. Let me know if you hear anything I need to know."

"I will." Cooper disconnected the call and then stared out across the front yard as his mind worked overtime. *If Nicole was telling the truth, then who the heck—*

Her ex?

Cooper pulled his phone out and called Reb back.

CHAPTER SIXTEEN

It was late when she looked about the kitchen at Trudy and Sally Ann. They were still here and would have stayed all night if she let them. Gert had to open the diner up early because she started serving breakfast at six and then lunch and closed at three. And Darlene had to get her daughter tucked in for the night. She couldn't express how she felt about this group of women who had stepped in to rescue her.

"I don't know how to thank you all. I was overwhelmed and can't tell you what seeing y'all walk into my kitchen meant to me."

"It was the least we could do," Trudy said. "We can't have you thinking our town is full of vandals and women who've lost all sense where men are concerned."

There was no illusions of what woman Trudy was talking about. And that was exactly what she'd been thinking about as she'd been cleaning her destroyed kitchen before they had arrived to change her opinion. Tears burned in her eyes.

"You all have helped me not load my goats up and head out of town."

Trudy had turned out a lot more spunky than Beth had first realized. "I can tell you, I'm not supposed to be jumping to conclusions and all that, but I'm ready to kick me some spoiled girl rear end."

Those words coming from the small older woman startled an unexpected laugh out of Beth. "I have to agree. I just can't fathom why even Nicole would go this far."

Sally Ann frowned. "Are you sure you don't want to come stay with me in town at the bed-and-breakfast? Or I can stay here with you tonight. I've got my shotgun and I can scare anybody off."

Trudy agreed. "The B&B might be the best option. We don't need Sally Ann shooting one of your cute goats on accident."

"I'm fine. Really." She wasn't completely, but she wasn't going to be scared out of her house. She'd lock the doors and if there was any trouble, she knew Cooper and his family were just down the road.

Speaking of the Presleys, they were all outside, circled up and having a talk. After the ladies left with promises to return the next day to help finish up, she headed outside to see what the men were discussing.

"I don't like it," Marcus was saying.

"I don't either," she heard Cooper saying. "And that's why I'm staying here tonight, unless I can talk her into coming to the ranch house."

"Hey, fellas. You've all been wonderful but I'm not leaving. I've got the goats to take care of and y'all are just down the road."

Cooper did not look happy. "I'm not leaving here knowing you're in that house alone all night."

His brothers all crossed their arms and said

nothing. They just watched to see who would win this power of wills.

She might find Cooper Presley irresistible but she was not one to be told what she could and could not do. "Then stay if you must because I'm not leaving. Thanks so much, fellas, for all you've done. But now I'm beat and going in for the night." As hard as it was to think about spending the night alone tonight, she refused to be run out of her own home.

She had just entered the house when Cooper knocked on the door. She opened it, not sure what to expect.

"So, where am I going to sleep, Miss Too-Stubborn-For-Your-Own-Good?"

"The couch is a mess. I'd offer you a bedroom but you already know there is no furniture in them. I have blankets but that's it."

"I'll sleep on the floor if I have to. I just want to make sure you're safe."

Tension radiated between them. "I can take care of myself," she snapped, the tension getting the better of her.

Cooper stepped forward and pulled her into his arms. Instantly her breathing sped up and she stiffened. She fought to hold her emotions at bay.

"Beth, you're one stubborn woman. Humor me— let me be here for you. It doesn't mean you're weak. Or that you're giving up your independence. I just want to make sure you're okay. You're so tense I just want to be here so at least you can relax and hopefully get some sleep."

She was tense. And despite all the women and cowboys wandering around and helping her all evening, her nerves were knotted up so tightly she wasn't sure they'd ever loosen up.

Looking up at him, she felt a rush of something so strong it made her wonder why she was fighting him. "I am not afraid of Nicole. She did this to my place in hopes that I'll be afraid. Not happening. If she shows back up here, she'll be surprised to know that I might be small but I'm not incapable of taking care of myself."

Cooper's eyes flashed with something that took her a moment to put her finger on, but realized it was uncertainty that she saw in his eyes. "What?" she asked, knowing there was something he wasn't telling her.

"Reb said that Nicole seemed truly surprised about your house being ransacked. There is a very good possibility she didn't do this."

"What? Then who…" Her words trailed off as she saw what he was thinking. "I'm too far away from Houston. He wouldn't—"

"Reb is running some checks on him. And Beth, he's gone off-grid. He moved out of his duplex last week and just disappeared."

She stared at him and a shiver raced down her spine.

Cooper hated to tell her what he'd learned. He should have told her earlier but she was just starting to look more like herself while working with all the women cleaning the house. He had hated the thought of just this, seeing that stricken look on her face. "Are you sure this guy didn't hurt you?"

Her eyes flashed. "No, he didn't hurt me. I wouldn't let him hurt me. I told you that."

Something wasn't right, he realized. He smoothed her hair, feeling the tension so tight in her that she was stiff. She might want to appear to be tough and she was, to a point, but she also had a vulnerable side and this jerk of an ex had done something bad enough to send her two hundred miles to start a new life.

"Then why do you tense up like this when he's mentioned?"

"Because he didn't physically harm me, but he toyed with me, had me questioning my own judgment and feeling weak. And there was the threat that he might snap and do something. And that disgusted me. At myself."

"At yourself?"

"I don't want to be afraid."

"But you are. And that's why you get so tense."

She sighed and nodded. "He did that to me. And if what you say is true, and he's here somewhere and he did this…"

"I'm not going to let anything happen to you. My

brothers are on watch and so is Reb. If he's out there, we'll find him. There is still a possibility that Nicole is a good liar and that she is the one who did this. Or it could be some vandal looking for loot. No matter who it is, I'm going to stick around as long as you'll let me."

She leaned her head against his shoulder and nodded. He got the impression she was only doing it because she was tired. "Thanks," she said after too short of a moment.

He liked having her in his arms. Couldn't stand the idea of her being upset. It was a new feeling he wasn't used to, this wanting her here in his arms all the time. He felt a little powerless against the strong pull of longing to keep her close.

Beth slept restlessly despite knowing that Cooper was sleeping on the floor in the other room. After learning the news that Scott had disappeared, she had felt those weak emotional feelings that she'd felt at her lowest when he'd been harassing her. She couldn't stand it.

Cooper sensed her state of mind. Sometimes she thought he could read her mind. It was uncanny, irritating, and comforting at the same time.

Unable to sleep, around two, she slipped into her housecoat and moved quietly into the kitchen. She almost screamed when she walked into the dark room and saw the shadow of a man leaning against the counter, holding something in his hands. "Cooper, you startled me."

"Sorry. Couldn't sleep and thought I'd make a cup of coffee. I didn't want to turn the lights on, because I didn't want to scare anyone away."

He spoke in quiet tones that were soothing in the darkness. "I see. I couldn't sleep either."

"There's more coffee in the pot if you want some."

She wasn't a big coffee drinker, enjoying the milder tones of tea but tonight was not a night for mild. "Thanks." She moved past him and poured herself a cup. "It's a wonder this didn't get smashed in the break-in."

"Probably just an oversight. You had it shoved in

that corner so I figure it's not an everyday habit you've acquired, like me."

She leaned against the counter, leaving space between them in the darkness. "No. I drink it sometimes. But I usually have a protein and veggie shake in the mornings. And maybe a cup of green tea with honey mid-morning if I need a pick-me-up."

"I'm not sure I get the vegetables in a shake thing but I can see you as a tea drinker. Fits your personality."

"Hey, spinach in a strawberry and protein shake is delicious. And power packed. Kale and sweet potatoes are good too."

Even in the darkness, she could sense his upper lip curling. "I am not drinking a sweet potato."

She laughed, for the first time since walking into her torn-up home. "Real men only eat sweet potatoes?"

"I guess—something like that. All I know is I'm feeling a little queasy at the mere thought of it."

She chuckled softly. "Thanks for the laugh. I needed it."

"I'll stand on my head if that will help you laugh."

"Although it makes for an interesting picture in my mind and a tempting offer, I don't think it's necessary."

They drank their coffee in silence. Just the warm cup between her palms was a comforting feeling.

Cooper here was a comforting feeling.

"Well, I better go back to bed." She walked past him and paused. Then she kissed his cheek. "Thanks."

"Anytime," he said as she left him there and went back to bed.

The ladies, true to their word—those who could—showed up the next morning. Cooper left around six, to head home and shower and then help with the roundup. He knew the ladies would be there around eight. At least that was his guess.

"They're early risers and if they didn't think they'd be disturbing you, they'd be here by seven." He gave her a quick kiss on the forehead and then brushed his lips across hers.

He'd been right. They were knocking on her door

at eight sharp.

"Coffee's on the counter if you need it." She felt much stronger today than she had the day before. The couches had dried some but needed another round of cleaning.

Trudy glared at the couch. "I'm calling the professionals to come out today to really get that gunk out of that pretty upholstery. I don't trust that machine we're using. I think it's old as dirt and I'm going to inform the store owner he needs a new one."

"Good idea." Sally Ann had cotton swabs to clean gunk out of the seams between the shiplap board on the walls. Thankfully it was only in one spot that ketchup had been squirted on the actual wall or they would have been working on that job for days.

There was a loud knock on the front door and Beth went to open it. She was startled when a very angry Nicole barged past her and into the room. She glared at everyone.

"How dare you send the cops to blame me for your house being vandalized. I would never do something like—"

"Calm down, Nicole," she broke into the tirade. She was really tired of the woman's temper tantrums.

"I will not—"

"Yes you will, young lady," Sally Ann said as she and Trudy moved to stand on either side of Beth. "I once wouldn't have thought you would stoop to something so low but these days, with the way you've been misbehaving, you're the first person I thought about when I heard poor Beth's home had been torn up."

Nicole's mouth dropped open but before she could say anything or before Beth could say anything, Trudy started in on Nicole.

"She's absolutely right. I've been astonished and dismayed by your behavior. I was concerned for you. Sally and I even tried to hunt you down yesterday after that scene in the diner but you stormed out of there and disappeared. We went to your house and rode around town looking for your car, but you were nowhere to be seen. And then this."

Nicole looked a little deflated. "I didn't do this."

Shaking a finger at her, Trudy didn't look

convinced. "With all the hollering and spoiled brat antics you've been doing, trying to get my nephew to take you out again, it's not looking good to prove your innocence."

"She speaks the truth," Sally Ann agreed.

Nicole looked pale and she looked at Beth for the first time without animosity. "I may have been acting badly but I didn't do this." She glanced about the room.

Beth inhaled, thinking what to say. "I'd like to say I believe you, but I don't really know you, Nicole. I just know that from the moment I came to town, you've acted really ugly." Beth felt oddly bad, despite Nicole's rude behavior. "I even tried to talk to you about it but you wanted nothing to do with that. Many people stop going out after a couple dates. You date to figure out if you want to continue the relationship. If one doesn't want to continue for any reason, they end the dating. Cooper didn't do anything wrong. Unless there is something you aren't sharing with us. Is there?"

Nicole remained silent.

"Well, is there?" Trudy demanded.

"No," Nicole finally admitted. "I just really liked him. He's a great guy and after TJ ran off, I felt so low. When Cooper asked me out, I felt better and I fell hard. One date and I was hooked. But he didn't appreciate my openness about my feelings. I didn't know that until our third date when he dropped me. It hurt, you know. Really hurt."

She could understand falling quickly and hard for Cooper. The man was wonderful. So kind and strong and thoughtful. And sexy as all get-out—yes, there was that.

"And you think what you're doing to Cooper doesn't hurt?" Sally Ann asked, not the least bit sympathetic. "We've got all kinds of bad things happening to women in this world and they're just now starting to speak up and be heard and then we've got women like you, lying about a good man because he just didn't feel that special something that happens between a couple that draws them together to continue dating or to get married. That isn't something you can make happen, Nicole. You can't harass a man into loving you."

Trudy crossed her arms and was in her mother hen mode. "And other men watching you harass another man is not a great calling card for future suitors. Didn't your mother teach you anything?"

Beth bit her lip as she let the scene play out. If Nicole hadn't done this, and she was beginning to believe she hadn't, then that left Scott. And this was exactly something he would do. She hadn't told Cooper that he'd torn her place in Houston up once. He just hadn't done all the nasty condiments from the refrigerator everywhere. For some reason, that had felt like something a woman would do and so she'd felt more strongly that it was Nicole, an angry ex-girlfriend.

"You are all right. I'm figuring that out. But, you have to believe me, I didn't do this."

"I believe you," Beth said at last.

Trudy and Sally Ann swung to face her.

"*You do?*" Trudy gasped.

"I agree," Sally Ann said and gave Beth a gentle squeeze on her upper arm.

"Oh good," Nicole said, tearfully. "I'm so sorry. Thank you for believing me."

Trudy, not quite ready to let her off the hook, shot her nose in the air. "It doesn't mean you're off the hook. Sheriff Reb hasn't said he believes you. Your actions count, young lady, and right now your actions have you in hot water. I have been worried about you but also upset with you. So, I'm a little confused about how to feel right now."

Beth laid a hand on Trudy's shoulder. "It's okay, Trudy. This has been hard on everyone. My suggestion, Nicole, is that you get over this grudge you have against Cooper. Let it go. And move on. And unless the sheriff finds evidence that you've just lied to us, then I won't be filing charges against you."

Nicole swallowed hard and looked upset. "I will. I don't know what I was thinking. I'll apologize to him. I'll go see if I can find him."

They watched her leave and Beth couldn't believe it. "Wow. What a mess."

"A hot mess," Trudy snapped. "I'm so mad I could pull my hair out."

Sally Ann laughed. "Well, don't do that. Just let steam off and then move on. Maybe she has learned a lesson." The older lady squinted at Beth. "So that means if she didn't do this, then who did?"

Beth sighed. "Well, I have my suspicions."

"You do?" Trudy looked at her in shock and Sally Ann too.

"I'm hoping I'm wrong." Beth frowned. "Truth is, Cooper isn't the only one with an angry ex not ready to stop dating."

CHAPTER SEVENTEEN

Beth went to Reb's office later in the afternoon to see whether he'd found anything else out and to also talk to him about Scott.

"We have a photo of him and my deputies are on the lookout for him around here. I've shared the photo with a few people around town who see a lot of flow, like Gert. Do you have a photo of him? If so, share it with anyone you think could be on the lookout. It might not be him but after what Cooper shared with me and what you've shared with me, my gut tells me this is our man."

"Yeah, my gut tells me the same thing."

"I think it would be a good idea for you to not be alone out there. Or maybe come to town and stay at the B&B or with Trudy."

Beth had had it. "I'm not leaving, Reb. I ran once. Came here and it was a great decision. But if Scott thinks he's scaring me and going to make me run again, he's wrong. Let me know if you find out anything. You can reach me at my place." She turned and left. Fury had her trembling on the inside as it had hit while standing there talking with Reb. She was not a victim.

"Beth, listen to reason," Reb called from the doorway of his office.

She turned back to him. "If he's going to come after me, then I'll be right where he can find me. So, I guess you and your team better figure out how to catch him when he comes."

She was at her place, getting Milly and Tilly ready for an afternoon photo shoot. The light was going to be great today—not too hot, not too bright, but just right. And she needed something to keep her busy. As she'd expected, Cooper's truck roared into her driveway about an hour after she got home. He'd been out working cattle, so she figured it would take him that long to get the call from Reb and to ride in from where ever he was working and get here to her place. She didn't turn around when she heard gravel crunching as he came to a screeching halt. Then the door slammed and she could imagine him storming across her yard in his chaps and boots and wearing fury for an expression.

"What are you thinkin', Beth?"

She was holding Milly and had half of her daisy-dotted dress on the little goat. She turned. "That I am done running. That's what."

"You're not stayin' here alone. I won't hear of it."

"Then stay. I didn't tell you to leave. But I also don't want to be responsible for putting you in danger."

He scoffed. "I'm not scared of this pansy who gets his kicks out of harassing women. I'd planned on staying and Reb talking you into moving into the B&B with Sally Ann and her shotgun."

"I'm staying here. So what if you teach me how to use a shotgun? I checked and Uncle Howard left one in the gun case. There's even a note on it that says he left it for me."

Cooper's temper simmered down a little. "That's a good idea."

"I thought so. Although, he might have moved on. This might have been his parting shot at me for humiliating him, as he called it."

"Maybe, but I don't think so." Cooper kicked the dirt in frustration. "Well, take whatever photos you can in an hour while I make some calls to my dad and brothers. And Reb. And then you're having a shotgun lesson."

The week went slow for Beth. There were no signs of Scott but they were pretty certain that it was him. He'd used a credit card in a nearby town and Reb felt that that hadn't been a coincidence that he was so close. But that wasn't why the week dragged on so slow. It was because she had an amazing, gorgeous cowboy living in her house. Trudy had brought a blowup bed to the house and put it in the extra bedroom for him, but half the time she found him in the kitchen or sleeping on the living room couch. He could hear better from that room.

That might have been true but it also put him more in her path and it was getting harder and harder to stay away from him.

She'd laid down the law when he came that night to stay and had told him there would be no hanky-panky just because he was living in her house for a few days. He'd immediately pulled her into his arms and kissed her until her knees were mush and she had no breath left.

"I can live for now without the hanky-panky but that right there was just a simple kiss."

There was nothing simple about any of his kisses and especially that one, which was meant to be a statement. *And oh my, was it ever.*

"Some kissing," she had agreed to, because yes, drat it all, she was a weak woman where his kisses were concerned.

On the fourth night, he came into her room and shook her. "Wake up, Beth. Shane texted me that it's time to rodeo. We've got a visitor."

"Shane? How does he know?" She sat up, fully awake.

"One of the brothers has been staked out in the trees across the pasture every night with a pair of night vision goggles. He's letting everyone else know right now that we're about to rodeo. Come on, let's get you away from the windows." He led her into the broom closet and opened the door. "Get inside."

"I'm not going in there."

"Yes, you are. I'm going outside and I want you safe." He kissed her quickly on the lips and pushed her inside.

She went, only because he was going to have backup and she didn't want to get in the way. And she hated to admit it but she might do just that.

Cooper's adrenaline was spiked to its limit as he eased

out the back door onto the porch. After sending Shane a text "Where?", he found the creep was still at the front of the house. After moving off the porch, he walked slowly to the edge of the house and waited. He wanted this guy. Wanted to sink his fist into his jaw for scaring Beth but mostly he wanted him off the streets.

After a minute, he heard the heavy footfalls of the guy. The instant he came around the corner of the house and Cooper saw his face Cooper knew it was Scott. The weasel. Cooper didn't give him time to flee as he slammed his fist dead center of the jerk's face. Cooper wasn't normally a violent man but he'd never run away from a fight. And this was a very satisfying crunch.

Scott yelled, grabbed his nose as he fell backward, and hit the ground, screaming like a newborn baby needing a bottle.

Cooper grabbed for him, hauled him up off the ground like he would a heifer and flipped him to his stomach.

"What are you doing?" Scott yelled. "Are you

crazy?"

"Me? You're the one who lost your mind when you started stalking Beth." Cooper was one of the best at tying a calf and he hadn't paused as Scott talked. He had tugged a small rope from where he'd placed it each night, sticking slightly from his front pocket, and he had Scott's hands tied together in seconds as he grabbed a leg, yanked his foot back and tied his foot to his hands. Only then did he remove his knee from Scott's back, step back and relax. Scott continued to yell and Milly, Tilly, and all the other goats yelled with him.

"Don't look like you need any help, little brother," Shane drawled, coming to stand beside him.

"Nope, I've got this one. Thanks for the heads-up."

Shane laughed. "You're welcome. It was an honor to help out your lady."

"She's not your lady." Scott yelled.

"Hey, watch him while I go let *my* lady out of the broom closet." He grinned and jogged toward the house.

Beth met him on the porch. "I heard noise and I couldn't help it. I had to come out. Did you get him?"

He grinned. "I got him. But to be honest, I think you could have taken that one down."

She laughed and threw her arms around his neck. "Thanks. But I have to admit that I'm glad I didn't have to try." And then she kissed him tenderly. "Thank you for being here for me."

He looked into her eyes and he knew in his heart that this was where he was meant to be.

"Beth, I'm going to tell you straight up that I love you. And I'm not ever going to let anything happen to you. But I'm also not going to rush you. And you can tell me to get lost and I'd have a hard time doing it, but I would. I'd leave you alone in peace if you could tell me you didn't love me too. I'm not going to chase you down and throw fits. I'd honor your wishes. I would—"

"Would you just kiss me? I'm never letting you go, cowboy."

"Seriously?"

"I'm seriously going to hurt you if you don't kiss me."

He laughed and swept her into his arms. "Well, darlin', I'm here to please." And then he lowered his lips to hers.

EPILOGUE

"Don't you look all spiffy in your pink dress," Cooper crooned as he lifted Tilly into his arms.

"Ooh, too cute to miss. Hold her a little closer," Beth said from behind the camera. She was doing a new calendar shoot and Cooper had just come in from working at the ranch. He wore his chambray denim shirt, worn jeans, and butter soft caramel toned chaps. He looked good and sent her insides two-stepping from simply looking at him. Hers. He was hers and she still couldn't believe it.

They'd been married for three months and those months had been full of laughter and loving that had her insides humming thinking about it. She focused on the shot though, of her hunky husband and Tilly, who was sporting a hot pink sundress. The man practically treated her goats like they were kids, real kids. Ready for the shot she wanted, she met her husband's green gaze. Her insides danced with delight and longing and she watched Cooper look adorable and sexy with the small goat snuggled in his strong arms.

His eyes danced with mischief as he played along. "Like this?" He scooted the tiny goat closer and immediately got a head-butt to the jaw. He laughed while Beth snapped multiple shots.

He cocked his head to the side. "You knew she was going to do that."

Beth giggled. "I cannot tell a lie. But I sure got a fabulous photo. I'm going to put it in my file for a Cowboys of Ransom Creek calendar." She couldn't help teasing him and was still holding out hope of talking the handsome brothers into the idea. So far, they hadn't budged on their firm no.

Now, her gaze locked with her husband's she watched him set Tilly on the ground and take a step toward her. The gleam in his eye had her snapping another picture. He grinned and reached for her, causing her to laugh as he nuzzled her neck and held her close.

"This is the snuggling I've been thinking about all day."

She managed to hang onto her camera with one hand as she wrapped her arms around him and enjoyed the feel of his lips on her skin. "Me too. But you sure are cute with my goats. Are you sure you won't let me use you in my calendar? Just one shot. That one was perfect."

He stopped kissing her and lifted his head slightly. "Are you really serious?"

"I really am." She smiled, giving him an imploring look while holding her breath in hopes that he would say yes. "It would be so fun."

His brows met. "If you're sure, then go for it. But you know good and well I am not going to hear the end of this from my brothers."

She squealed and yanked him close in her excitement. "Thank you. And you can handle a little teasing. I adore you."

And she did. How had she been so lucky to run from one bad situation and end up here in his arms, with this life with him? She didn't know but felt blessed beyond measure.

"I'm so happy, Cooper." She kissed him long and hard, all the emotions she was feeling welling up and overflowing. He held her tight and joined into the kiss with gusto.

After a moment he chuckled and pulled back to look at her. "If I'd known me taking a picture with a goat would make you this happy I'd have already done it."

She laughed. "No, silly. That's only part of it. It's everything, our life together and...all of this," she paused, embraced by the enormity of what they'd found together.

He gently cupped her face with his hands. "I get it. I feel the same way. I'm so thankful you moved to town and we found each other. I love you and am the luckiest man alive because you love me."

She sighed. "You are a romantic, Cooper Presley."

He winked. "For you, I certainly am. I'm promising to be romantic with you as long as there is breath in my lungs. And I'm praying the good Lord gives me a hundred years of lovin' you. More if He sees fit, but I figure a hundred is stretching it."

She laughed, huskily. "It sounds like a great plan to me."

Cooper's lips hitched, his eyes darkening as he leaned her back into a dip and covered her lips with his.

A sigh escaped her as she let his love fill her with warmth, happiness and joy. Joy she had only dreamed of a few months ago.

Now, their future stretched before them sparkling with wonder and more kisses.

A lifetime of kisses. Of loving. Of sweet, sweet love.

Excerpt from

SHANE: THE COWBOY'S JUNK-STORE PRINCESS

Cowboys of Ransom Creek, Book Four

CHAPTER ONE

Reese Emory griped the steering wheel of her rental as she felt the wheels of the small car slide on the icy road. It was dark outside and she still had a few miles to go before she reached Ransom Creek and her Aunt Sally Ann's junk store.

"Reese, are you still there?" From her cell phone, her friend Lila's voice rang out in the dark interior of the car. From her cozy, warm apartment in Seattle she was trying to keep Reese company on the dark road.

"Sorry, I was concentrating on the road. It's getting slick. I wasn't expecting to come to Texas and get involved in an ice storm. Especially since I haven't driven a car in almost a year." Reese didn't need a car in the city. She took the train into the office every day-or had, until now, after taking a leave of absence. Trying not to feel depressed smiled, it was after all proven that smiling was good for you. Lifted you up even when you weren't particularly happy. The jury was still out on that as far as she was concerned. "But I'm managing." She was talking as much about managing the slick road as she was talking about managing her life right now.

"It's a sign," Lila cooed. "You need to turn that car around and get back here. I still don't get why you packed up and tossed in the towel so easy. Mason will be back and you know it. He's crazy about you."

"*He's* the one who wanted to take a break. Lila, it was not fun sitting there in that restaurant thinking he was going to propose to me and instead he was breaking up with me. And knowing that everyone in the office knows he broke it off...makes it all the more embarrassing." It had been humiliating actually. And then she was expected to walk back into work the next day as if nothing had happened. As if she and her boss hadn't been in a relationship that she'd believed had a future. A relationship and future that he'd decided he needed a break from. Just thinking about it irritated her. How had she been so blind.

Because you wanted to be.

She frowned. Sometimes she hated the voice in her head because it spoke the truth. But, it had been a little late on revealing that truth to her and that made her hate the sanctimonious voice in her head all the more.

Lila sighed on the other end of the country. "True, I'm sorry. But what am I supposed to do here on this end when I go into the office and you're not here?"

"You'll be fine. If you need me I'm just a phone call away." As her assistant, Lila had been with her on all of her designs. "Look at this as an opportunity for you to make an impression. Finish my projects and prove to them you're ready to step up. I told Mason you could do it."

"I don't want your job. I'd have an ulcer with your job."

The tires slipped again and Reese's fingers tightened on the steering wheel. "Look, Lila I resigned. If he's smart he will offer you the promotion and my job. Take it. Please don't feel a loyalty to me and pass up a career opportunity for yourself."

"I just don't like it."

Why was Ransom Creek out in the middle of nowhere? She'd told her Aunt Sally Ann that she was not interested in living in a small town with barely any phone service. But her aunt had always insisted she'd love it if she just gave it a chance. There was no chance of that happening but she'd needed a place to decompress.

Hide-the maddening voice interjected.

She'd needed a place to take some time off and it was the perfect time to spend a little time with her aunt.

"Are you still there?" Lila asked, her voice

crackling as the connection faded.

"I'm here, but I think we are about to lose connection and I probably better concentrate on this road before I end up in a ditch. Hugs, I'll call you tomorrow."

"What. Did you say tomorrow?"

"Yes." She got the word out and then the line was dead. Just then wheels hit a patch of ice, and her car went into a spin.

She did her best but after a stomach clenching ordeal and some squeals of fear, the car came to a halt in the ditch.

And she got a good right hook to the face from her air bag.

Shane Presley was driving home toward the ranch, pulling a load of cattle, when he saw the car skidding out of control in the oncoming lane. He slowed, ready to hit the ditch if he needed to if the driver was unable to regain control. But, instead he had to watch as the out of control car ended up in the ditch.

Many folks in Texas didn't handle icy roads too well. It was a fact. He hoped the people, or person in the car was okay. He got the truck stopped and then hurried as best that he could from the truck and across the icy grass. This was one of the coldest Decembers he'd remembered in a while and he knew on the interstates that they were having people in the ditches. Country roads were worse, less traveled. Reaching the car, he grabbed the door and yanked it open. In the beam of his truck lights the driver's gleaming blonde hair was the first thing he saw.

"Are you alright?" he asked. When the driver turned to look at him Shane lost his train of thought. Big pale blue eyes. Dazed eyes that worried him. "Ma'am, are you alright?"

"My head hurts after getting sucker punched by my airbag. But I think I'm fine." She blinked hard as if trying to clear them.

"Maybe I need to check you out-*I mean*, make sure you're not hurt." Looking at her, unable to look away from her, he knelt down between the car door and the driver's seat.

"You have a cut." He lifted his hand and touched her cheek where he saw a slight cut. At the feel of her soft skin his pulse jumped erratically. Startled by his reaction to this woman he took her chin gently in his fingertips and studied her pert nose, spotting a slight trickle of blood. "Did the air bag hit you in the face?"

Her brow furrowed. "Yes." She touched her nose and flinched. "Owe. Does my nose look broken?"

He almost smiled, but knowing how bad this could have been for her wiped the temptation away. "No, it's not crooked so you're okay. But it got you good. I'm relieved it didn't hurt you worse. Is it hurting?"

"It's hurting some but I'll be fine. Thanks for stopping to help me. What is your name, please?"

"Shane Presley. You passed my ranch back there. I'm heading home with this truck load of cold cattle. I promise I'm a good guy. You don't have anything to be afraid of."

She smiled and his gut clenched. "I figured that out. If you weren't a good guy I didn't want to be afraid of you, or to have to kick you or hurt you. Especially when you are being so helpful."

She wasn't afraid, he realized. Teasing, and irritated at her situation, but not afraid. "I'm not someone you should be afraid of but you might need to be a little leery of strangers in the dark."

She massaged her forehead, her pretty eyes glinting in the light. "Right now, I'm more interested in getting out of this ditch. Out of the cold, and to my aunt's house."

"Who is your aunt?"

"Sally Ann Riggs, she owns the junk store in town."

This was Sally Ann's niece. "I know Sally Ann. I'm Shane Presley. She said you were coming. Made me and all my brothers promise to come by and meet you." All of them had known instantly that Sally Ann was hoping to fix one of them up with her niece. He hadn't been too excited about the prospect but now, she had his full attention.

Her pretty lips tugged downward. "Presley. I should have known."

He frowned now. "What does that mean?"

"You're one of the "good lookin' hunk of

cowboy" as my aunt always puts it when she is talking to me about you and your brothers. Five of you, right?"

He laughed. "Yes, five. And while I appreciate your aunt giving me and my brothers such a fine compliment, I don't think you're impressed."

"I'm cold. And my head hurts. And I'm taking the fifth on the other. Could you by chance give me a ride to her house or pull me out of this ditch?"

"I'll give you a ride and then come back and get the car. Grab what you need. Or point me in the right direction and I'll get it."

She pushed the button and he heard the trunk click. He waited while she grabbed her purse and her coat. He stood then and held his hand out to assist her from the car. The sleet had started coming down more and he didn't want her falling. Her shoes, when he saw them, didn't give him confidence in the situation. The heels on her high heeled boots looked more like ice picks. Long ice picks.

"Are you planning on walking in the ice in those?"

"I'm going to try. I wasn't expecting the storm of the century to roll in after I got off the airplane."

He wrapped his hand securely around hers, it was cold, but a warmth filled him, hummed through him like happy bees swarming a honeysuckle bush. He swallowed hard, unnerved by her touch. "Steady," he murmured as she took a step.

She immediately slipped on the ice-covered grass.

"Oh," she said, her voice wobbly as her ankles. She gripped his hand while slinging out her other hand to grasp the top of the door. Still, with her feet sliding on the ice if he hadn't steadied her she would have gone down.

"This could be tricky," she muttered.

"You might say that," he agreed as their gazes held. Her eyes that appeared almost silver in the truck light.

"Is this storm supposed to last long?"

He hated to give her the bad news. "Maybe. It's supposed to be a hard winter. And seeing as how the last few have barely had a freeze at all, we really need a good hard freeze. Clears out some of the bugs that bother both human and cattle. So, as uncomfortable as the ice is we're glad to see it."

She bit her lip. "Then I guess it's out of the equation for me to wait in my car until the sun comes out."

"That's a fair observation."

"Okay then we better get going because it may take us till spring for me to get to your truck with these heels on."

He chuckled. "No, ma'am it won't." And then he scooped her into his arms, gave her a bounce so she instantly flung her arms around his neck.

She squealed, "What are you doing?"

"Getting you out of this weather before we both catch pneumonia."

"Oh, okay. I'll bow to your judgement if you think you can carry me through this."

He grinned at her and felt a twinge in his chest looking at her up close. "I've carried more calves than you know through worse than this and we made it fine." He stepped easy, making sure he didn't fall flat on his butt after making that statement. But despite his thick coat and her, not-thick-enough coat he was enjoying the feel of her in his arms. To her credit she held on to him with her arms without squeezing him to death, not that he would have minded. And she didn't say anything, letting him concentrate.

The sleet stung against his cheeks and she ducked her face to the crook of his neck to keep it from hitting her. After several steps he made it to the slippery pavement and chose to put her into the truck from his side in order to minimize the chances of them both going down in a heap on the icy road. "You'll have to push that console up in the middle and then you can slide across the bench seat to the passenger side. This is our safest bet on not busting it." He set her down on the seat.

She chuckled. "I can do that. Thanks"

He tipped his icy hat. "You're more than welcome. Now get warm and I'll grab your suitcase."

He closed the door and strode carefully back to her trunk to retrieve the suitcase. It felt like it weighed two hundred pounds. *What did she have inside that thing?*

Hauling it by the side handle he strode to the truck and placed it into the bed of the truck. The cows moved slightly but said nothing as he glanced their direction.

"I'm sorry about keeping your cattle out longer than you probably planned. I feel bad for them."

"Don't. They're made a thick skin and are huddled together so they have warmth going on between them. They're fine."

"If you say so."

"It's true." He had them moving down the road in seconds. He shot her a glance. "Are you okay?"

"I think. My head hurts though. I guess I should be thankful I didn't get a nose bleed or a broken nose."

"Probably. But you may have some bruising."

"I can deal with that."

"What brings you to Ransom Creek? Your aunt said you had gotten engaged. We didn't figure you'd be around after we heard that news."

"I, just felt like it was time to come see her. She's been after me for so long and I just felt like the timing was right."

She seemed to fidget in the seat and since the interior light had now gone out all he had was the light from the dashboard. He sensed there was more to the story but he decided it was none of his business. "I'll just drive up to the ranch and unhitch these cattle if you don't mind."

"Sure. Do what you need to do. I'm the one hitching a ride. I'll try to call my aunt and let her know what's happened. I lost reception back there."

"That happens. Especially in bad weather." He decided to back up to the cattle pen and let them out of the trailer. "I'll be right back." He climbed out into the storm, the ice harder now, pelting him on the cheeks. A few minutes later he climbed back inside, his pulse instantly spiked when their eyes met. The woman had affected him. "Did you reach Sally Ann?"

She didn't say anything at first, staring at him then she blinked and a cute crease formed between her brows. "Yes, and she was so relieved that you had found me."

He just bet she was. Sally Ann was his aunt Trudy's best friend and if she could have her niece marry him or one of his brothers that would fulfill her dream. Only problem was Reese was engaged although he didn't see a ring on her finger.

"I'm glad she was happy. Now, let's get you to her place."

"Thanks, these roads are going to be worse before they get better. Are you sure you need to be out in this too much longer? It looks like it's getting worse."

Was she kidding? "Yes. I'm not going to drop you off on the side of the road just so I don't have to drive on icy roads. If you're worried about being out then you could stay here at the house. My dad's in there and would be glad to offer you a room. But, your aunt has been pushing to have you come visit for so long that there is no way I'm going to be the one who keeps her from seeing you tonight. I kind of like the idea of being the one who makes her happy by getting you there tonight."

She looked thoughtful. "I see your point. I'll admit that I'm ready to get there too."

"Then you will be and I get to be everyone's hero." He watched her eyes light up in the dim light. That funny feeling nudged into his chest again. She was engaged so was off limits but there was no denying the buzz of attraction he was feeling. Didn't matter though, as he shoved disappointment aside knowing she was engaged. What was wrong with him anyway?

"You certainly are mine. Didn't you recently have a brother get married?"

"Yes, I did. Cooper. He married Beth about three months ago. When are you tying the knot?" He concentrated on the road but hadn't been able to stop the question. He was too interested. Besides that, if she said the date then that would finalize the fact that she was not a free woman for him to be interested in. Just his luck.

"Well, um, the date isn't nailed down just yet."

The fact that some man had proposed then not set the date with the pretty blonde had him wondering what was wrong with the man. "Is he short a few straws in his haystack?" he asked, his question blunt as the thought that had hit him wrong.

"What does that mean?" she said, a startled laugh escaping her.

"Just what I asked. Is something wrong with your

fiancé? Seems to me if he put a ring on your finger he would have nailed down a date. But then, I didn't see a ring on your finger which leads me to really wonder if he's missing a few screws up top." He risked a quick glance at her seeing the glint of anger in her intriguing eyes before he focused back on the road.

"Not that it's any of your business, but I forgot to put my ring on before I got on the plane. And Mason is a *very* smart man."

"Very? If you say so," he scoffed, feeling irritable. Why was he needling her like this? It was none of his business. Still, he couldn't help taking another jab, "I think that could be debated."

He felt her frown in the darkness even without taking his eyes off the road. He wouldn't fault her for slapping him for being so rude. But maybe that was what he was hoping for. Maybe he needed some sense slapped into him, because no matter how he sliced and diced it, he was attracted to Reese Emory. And he wished to high heavens she'd come to town a couple of months ago before the invisible ring had been put on her finger.

More Books by Debra Clopton

Star Gazer Inn of Corpus Christi Bay
What New Beginnings are Made of (Book 1)

Sunset Bay Romance
Longing for Forever (Book 1)
Longing for a Hero (Book 2)
Longing for Love (Book 3)
Longing for Ever-After (Book 4)
Longing for You (Book 5)
Longing for Us (Book 6)

Texas Brides & Bachelors
Heart of a Cowboy (Book 1)
Trust of a Cowboy (Book 2)
True Love of a Cowboy (Book 3)

New Horizon Ranch Series
Her Texas Cowboy (Book 1)
Rafe (Book 2)
Chase (Book 3)
Ty (Book 4)
Dalton (Book 5)
Treb (Book 6)
Maddie's Secret Baby (Book 7)
Austin (Book 8)

Turner Creek Ranch Series
Treasure Me, Cowboy (Book 1)
Rescue Me, Cowboy (Book 2)
Complete Me, Cowboy (Book 3)
Sweet Talk Me, Cowboy (Book 4)

Cowboys of Ransom Creek
Her Cowboy Hero (Book 1)
The Cowboy's Bride for Hire (Book 2)
Cooper: Charmed by the Cowboy (Book 3)
Shane: The Cowboy's Junk-Store Princess (Book 4)
Vance: Her Second-Chance Cowboy (Book 5)
Drake: The Cowboy and Maisy Love (Book 6)
Brice: Not Quite Looking for a Family (Book 7)

Texas Matchmaker Series
Dream With Me, Cowboy (Book 1)
Be My Love, Cowboy (Book 2)
This Heart's Yours, Cowboy (Book 3)
Hold Me, Cowboy (Book 4)
Be Mine, Cowboy (Book 5)
Operation: Married by Christmas (Book 6)
Cherish Me, Cowboy (Book 7)
Surprise Me, Cowboy (Book 8)
Serenade Me, Cowboy (Book 9)
Return To Me, Cowboy (Book 10)
Love Me, Cowboy (Book 11)
Ride With Me, Cowboy (Book 12)
Dance With Me, Cowboy (Book 13)

Windswept Bay Series
From This Moment On (Book 1)
Somewhere With You (Book 2)
With This Kiss (Book 3)
Forever and For Always (Book 4)
Holding Out For Love (Book 5)
With This Ring (Book 6)
With This Promise (Book 7)
With This Pledge (Book 8)
With This Wish (Book 9)
With This Forever (Book 10)
With This Vow (Book 11)

About the Author

Bestselling author Debra Clopton has sold over 2.5 million books. Her book OPERATION: MARRIED BY CHRISTMAS has been optioned for an ABC Family Movie. Debra is known for her contemporary, western romances, Texas cowboys and feisty heroines. Sweet romance and humor are always intertwined to make readers smile. A sixth generation Texan she lives with her husband on a ranch deep in the heart of Texas. She loves being contacted by readers.

Visit Debra's website at www.debraclopton.com

Sign up for Debra's newsletter at
www.debraclopton.com/contest/

Check out her Facebook at
www.facebook.com/debra.clopton.5

Follow her on Twitter at @debraclopton

Contact her at debraclopton@ymail.com

If you enjoyed reading *Cooper: Charmed by the Cowboy* I would appreciate it if you would help others enjoy this book, too.

Recommend it. Please help other readers find this book by recommending it to friends, reader's groups and discussion boards.

Review it. Please tell other readers why you liked this book by reviewing it on the retail site you purchased it from or Goodreads. If you do write a review, please send an email to debraclopton@ymail.com so I can thank you with a personal email. Or visit me at: www.debraclopton.com.

Made in the USA
Middletown, DE
03 December 2020